P9-DCD-894

"Tell me who you're running from."

"I don't know...I mean, I'm not..." They were so close, Josie was almost in Bart's arms. "You're trying to confuse me again."

More touching was involved as she peeled the shirt down off his shoulders, first to free his good right arm, then to slip it off his injured left. Though she tried not to stare, she couldn't help admiring his magnificent musculature. Nor could she ignore his flat stomach and the light dusting of hair that trailed down below the waist of his jeans.

Bart cupped her cheek, turned her face to his. "Someone hurt you," he said. "A man. Tell me."

"I'll get some ice packs for your arm."

"What's your name?"

"Josie Wales." She turned away.

He slowly pulled her head toward him. Then he brushed her mouth with his. Just a momentary touch. Even so, she shuddered at the sensation that was strangely erotic.

"I meant your *real* name...."

If only she knew....

Dear Reader,

I've always thought that if I were to move from Chicago, it would be to northern New Mexico. I love the look and the feel of the place—the brilliant sunny skies with a clear light that inspires me; the rugged landscapes that remind me of a past that I still romanticize as I did when I was a kid.

And so it was an exceptional pleasure for me to bring a bit of that romanticized past to my latest Harlequin Intrigue books. SONS OF SILVER SPRINGS—half brothers Bart, Chance and Reed—return to save the Curly-Q Ranch despite bitter memories of each other and their relationship with their father who is dying. In doing so, they not only find danger and the loves of their lives, but a new respect for family and tradition.

If you enjoy their ride, please let me know— P.O. Box 578297, Chicago, IL 60657-8297. Send an SASE for information on upcoming books.

Regards,

Patricia Rosemoor

Heart of a Lawman
Patricia Rosemoor

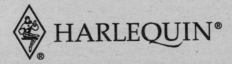

TORONTO • NEW YORK • LONDON
AMSTERDAM • PARIS • SYDNEY • HAMBURG
STOCKHOLM • ATHENS • TOKYO • MILAN • MADRID
PRAGUE • WARSAW • BUDAPEST • AUCKLAND

If you purchased this book without a cover you should be aware
that this book is stolen property. It was reported as "unsold and
destroyed" to the publisher, and neither the author nor the
publisher has received any payment for this "stripped book."

ISBN 0-373-22559-8

HEART OF A LAWMAN

Copyright © 2000 by Patricia Pinianski

All rights reserved. Except for use in any review, the reproduction or
utilization of this work in whole or in part in any form by any electronic,
mechanical or other means, now known or hereafter invented, including
xerography, photocopying and recording, or in any information storage
or retrieval system, is forbidden without the written permission of the
publisher, Harlequin Enterprises Limited, 225 Duncan Mill Road,
Don Mills, Ontario, Canada M3B 3K9.

All characters in this book have no existence outside the imagination of
the author and have no relation whatsoever to anyone bearing the same
name or names. They are not even distantly inspired by any individual
known or unknown to the author, and all incidents are pure invention.

This edition published by arrangement with Harlequin Books S.A.

® and TM are trademarks of the publisher. Trademarks indicated with
® are registered in the United States Patent and Trademark Office, the
Canadian Trade Marks Office and in other countries.

Visit us at www.romance.net

Printed in U.S.A.

An exclusive interview with
Harlequin Intrigue author Patricia Rosemoor!

Q: What was the first romance you ever read?
PR: It was called *Double Date* and I was in the third grade. I finished my schoolwork and pulled out my book, only to have Sister Ursula confiscate it disapprovingly because it was a "Senior" library book, and being only seven, I was supposed to have a "Juvenile" card. When she returned it the next day, she suggested I should start reading books about history instead.

Q: Where do you get your inspiration?
PR: Often from learning about real struggles of real people. Other times from subjects that concern me, especially when it comes to animal welfare.

Q: What do you feel is special about this particular series, SONS OF SILVER SPRINGS?
PR: In spending time in New Mexico to do the research, I met a family that has recently opened their ranch to vacationers in an effort to preserve their way of life. I felt honored that they allowed my husband and I to stay in their home and be part of their family for a few days. And in doing so, I learned a new respect for those who pursue traditional ways of life (hard work and simple pleasures) in lieu of big-city careers and amenities. I hope that my true appreciation is apparent in the SONS OF SILVER SPRINGS series.

To read the complete interview with Patricia Rosemoor, log on to our web site at www.romance.net.

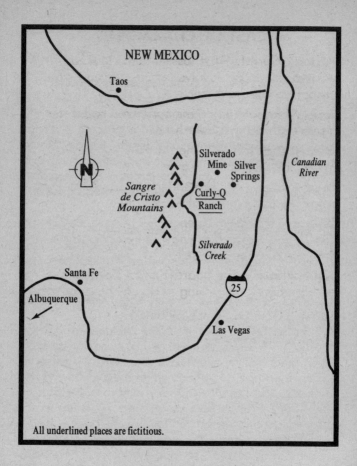

NEW MEXICO

Taos

Silverado
Mine

Silver
Springs

Canadian
River

Sangre
de Cristo
Mountains

Curly-Q
Ranch

Silverado
Creek

Santa Fe

Albuquerque

25

Las Vegas

All underlined places are fictitious.

CAST OF CHARACTERS

Barton Quarrels — The last thing the lawman wanted was to get involved with a woman who brought trouble with her.

Josie Wales — With no memory, how could she figure out who was after her?

Emmett Quarrels — Owner of the Curly-Q, Bart's father has secrets of his own.

Hugh Ruskin — The bartender was hostile to Josie when he didn't get what he wanted.

William "Billy Boy" Spencer — The new cowboy at the Curly-Q seemed to know more about Josie than she did about herself.

Tim Harrigan — The boarder at the Springs Bed and Breakfast was willing to do anything for Josie.

To research SONS OF SILVER SPRINGS,
my husband and I went straight to the source—
a ranch in New Mexico called Rancho Cañón Ancho,
a jewel set in canyon splendor along the Mora River.
We got more than we'd bargained for,
both in the background information I was seeking
and in hospitality. So I would like to thank
Bryan and Kathy Turner, a couple who really
ride for the brand and are keeping alive traditional
ranch life for their son, Ethan. Also thanks to
Kathy's mom, Betty Snow, who helped Kathy
feed and entertain us in true Southwestern fashion.

Prologue

He was still behind her!

Heedless of the dark, moonless night, of the winding, downhill road and rain-slicked pavement, of the clumsy vehicle at her command, she jammed the accelerator all the way to the floor.

As if bitten, the truck she had stolen leaped forward crazily and threatened to shoot straight off the road.

Palms sweaty, she white-knuckled the steering wheel…successfully wrestled the cumbersome old rattletrap around a hairpin curve and away from the sheer drop…darted her nervous gaze to the rearview mirror….

Nothing for a moment. Then she saw the twin beams make the turn, as well. The headlights seemed a bit more distant, but still they kept pace with her.

She held her breath, the only sounds filling her ears the rumble of the engine punctuated by worn wipers clack-clacking as they streaked across the windshield.

It came to her then that she would never be free of him. She'd tried everything in her power, and still he was there, a dark phantom, a portent of her future. What little she had left of one, for the distance between his headlights and the truck was closing.

He would never let her go. Never let her get away. *Never let her live.*

And she had no one to blame but herself.

Sickness welled in her as she acknowledged the fate that she had brought down on herself. Her chest tightened and the bitter taste of acid filled her mouth. Her eyelids stung as self-anger grew.

"No!"

She slapped the steering wheel so hard her palm stung. She wouldn't cry. Not now. Not after everything she'd endured.

But the tears flooded her eyes, and even as she swept around another downward curve, she dashed them away with a shaky hand. Only a second's inattention—that fast!—and the truck veered over, halfway into the oncoming lane. Before she could pull it back in line, her eyes filled again, this time with bright, blinding lights. The windshield wipers swept the image into focus: another vehicle heading straight for her.

An eighteen-wheeler, horn blaring!

Jerking the wheel was her second mistake. The old truck took on a life of its own, skated sideways over the slick pavement. Fear and adrenaline flooding her, she tried to keep her head. Steer into the skid. Brake gently.

Too late.

A tire grabbed the shoulder and spat gravel, while the rear end spun around and off solid ground into nothingness. Her heart skipped a beat as the rest of the truck followed. Flew without wings. For a second, she felt suspended....

Suddenly, a roller-coaster drop whipped her head into the side window and churned her stomach into her throat. Then turned *her* as the upended truck careened downward.

Free fall...

Touchdown.

The crash sent an explosion along her nerves, straight to her mind. She was straining against the seat belt, her voice catching as she tried to remember a prayer.

To escape the pain, she gladly entered the darkness....

Chapter One

Three miles out of the crumbling town of Silver Springs, Barton Quarrels pulled his four-by-four onto the washboard-dirt ranch road that would throw him back half a lifetime. Everything *looked* the same, he thought. Worn cedar and barbed wire fences. Yellowing grasses. A handful of mostly white-faced livestock grazing the high desert pasture.

What he feared was that everything would *be* the same.

His kids had been quiet all the way up from Albuquerque. Sullen, really. They'd get over it. Had to. He was doing this for them.

Well mostly, anyhow.

"Almost there," he told them. In an effort to engage them, to rustle some little enthusiasm where he knew there to be none, he asked, "So, after you get your stuff settled in your rooms, what do you want to do?"

"Nothing *to* do out here but count cows," Daniel mumbled.

"As I remember, you used to like that, 'cause it meant you were on a horse."

"That's when I was a kid."

"Yeah, right. I keep forgetting."

As far as Bart was concerned, sixteen was far from adulthood, but he needn't alienate Daniel more. The air between them already bristled with teenage hostility.

Bart stopped the vehicle at the pasture's barrier, and his son jumped out to open the metal pipe and wire gate. Daniel waited until his father had pulled through the opening before swinging the gate closed and clambering back into the passenger seat. The ritual was one repeated all over the ranch, whose nearly sixty thousand acres were broken down into manageable pastures.

Bart waited until they were once more on the prowl, past the scale house where cattle on the way to market were weighed before being shipped.

Then he tried making conversation again, this time with his daughter. "Hey, Lainey, honey, want to take some photographs around the place this afternoon?" Photography being her hobby.

He glanced in the rearview mirror to check out the twelve-year-old, whose attention was seemingly glued to those boring cows.

"Mom would hate this," she suddenly said, head churning forward, green eyes exactly like Sara's boring into the back of his neck. "She'd hate *you*, putting our home up for sale, making us move."

Bart tore his gaze from the mirror and put it back where it belonged—on the road. "Your mother didn't have a hateful bone in her body."

Unable to help gripping the steering wheel, he couldn't imagine ever completely erasing the pain of loss that burdened him.

"It's not too late, Dad," Lainey continued darkly. "The house didn't sell yet, so we can still go home...."

"The Curly-Q's gonna be our home now."

Ignoring the interruption, the girl insisted, "You can get your deputy's badge back and everything!"

Not that he'd really lost it in the first place.

Though he hadn't told his kids—he didn't want to raise their hopes—Bart had been smart enough to leave himself a safety net, just in case. He'd taken a long-term leave of absence and could go back to his old job as long as it remained vacant. The sheriff hadn't wanted to lose him and so had promised to stall things, to keep his spot open for several weeks, at least.

Just in case.

But even a city as small as Albuquerque had growing problems that made Bart's gut quake, not for himself, but for those he loved. He'd lost a wife to violence less than a year ago. He wasn't going to give up his kids, as well.

After his mother's death, Daniel had secretly joined a gang and had gotten into trouble defacing the high school with cans of spray paint. Bart wondered what he *hadn't* gotten caught at. While he'd made his son swear to quit the gang, he knew the promise he'd wrung out of the boy was illusory. Peer pressure would get him in the end and he'd be sneaking out with his friends again. It was only a matter of time unless Daniel was removed from the path of temptation.

And Bart was willing to do anything to protect his kids...even sell his soul.

He stared out at the devil's playground.

Rich, volcanic-based grasslands stretched around them as far as the eye could see. An optical illusion that plains gradually gave way to mountains. Though they were in the foothills of the Sangre de Cristo range, the foothills here were nearly seven thousand feet up.

Clear air. Piercing blue sky. A slice of heaven.

At least the land itself was....

They'd reached the piñon-and-ponderosa-pine-limned rimrock, their future spread out before them in all its splendor. The road here was dotted with dark green cedar, rusting scrub oak and the occasional grayish juniper bush.

The skin along Bart's spine prickled as he started the descent into the canyon cut by Silverado Creek, a fat ribbon of water that twisted and turned and rushed across the Curly-Q. Now its function was merely to appease thirsty cattle and to provide a water table for the surrounding grasslands, but at one time, the creek had serviced the mine, which lay farther up the canyon and connected to town by a road that was now all but impassable.

The first hairpin curve thrilled Bart as always, and, also as always, his stomach was ready for the second. What he wasn't prepared for was the state of the road, rutted by washout rains. The vehicle dipped and bounced its way down and red dust swirled around them. One spot was so bad that he found himself clenching his jaw so that he wouldn't bite his tongue.

What had his father been thinking—not taking care of the only road out before it became near-impossible to fix?

"I want you two to give this a chance," he said

as the house drew in sight. The sprawling adobe backed by a handful of outbuildings looked the same, too, he noted. "If you can't do it for me, then do it for your grandpa. Remember, we don't know how long he has."

Again, he glanced in the rearview mirror and caught the stricken expression Lainey was quick to hide.

"But Grandpa's got Uncle Reed and Uncle Chance," Daniel mumbled.

"*If* they decide to return."

Certainly neither Reed nor Chance were anywhere in sight. *No one was.* The handful of dusty old pickups—the newest of which had to be twenty years old—were ranch vehicles. Though he hadn't counted on his half-brothers agreeing to the deal, Bart experienced a moment's disappointment. Unsure that anything would drag Reed and Chance back into a situation they'd all hated, he'd still wondered what it would be like—the three of them riding herd together again. Maybe this time they were old enough to make peace with each other. Maybe they were wise enough to make it work.

But Reed and Chance didn't have families to think of. They had no reason to accept the devil's bargain the way he had.

Bart almost expected the old devil himself to be waiting for them as he pulled into the front yard and two yapping dogs rushed the truck. But Emmett Quarrels was nowhere in sight.

Instead, Felice Cuma, his father's housekeeper of nearly thirty years, flew out the front door, called the dogs and ordered them back to the barn. A smile of welcome flared fine lines around her dark eyes and full mouth. She had passed sixty, but Bart thought Felice was still a fine figure of a woman and couldn't imagine why she wasted her life keeping someone else's home when he was certain she could make one with a man of her own.

Lighting on Daniel as he unfolded all six feet of himself from the front passenger seat, Felice's eyes went wide. "*Chico,* you're a man now!"

Daniel grinned at Felice and rushed forward so they could give each other a big hug.

Arms folded across her chest, Lainey straggled behind. No smile loosened the tight grip that held her mouth in a flat line. Felice stepped out of Daniel's bear hug and stared at the girl, her hand going to her throat as if she'd just been struck speechless. And her dark eyes suddenly went luminous, Bart noted, as if she were holding back tears.

"Ah, *chica,*" Felice finally said, her voice trembling, "you've grown so beautiful. You look exactly like your sainted mama."

Lainey softened a little and allowed a hug, if not with her brother's open enthusiasm. Expression concerned, Felice sought Bart's gaze over his daughter's head. He shrugged and spread his hands in a helpless gesture.

"Hey, Felice," he said with affection.

"Mr. Bart. It's good to see you. You've stayed away far too long."

He knew Felice meant more than the last year and a half. That's how long it had been since he'd stepped foot on Curly-Q land—since well before Sara died. They'd driven their kids to the ranch for a visit every summer. Bart had sometimes stayed the night, but he'd always gone off on his own—usually

back to Albuquerque where he buried himself in
work—and then had to come back weeks later for
the three of them.

Sara really had been a saint, Bart thought, considering she'd been able to deal with the old tyrant
for weeks at a time, while Bart had trouble tolerating
his own father for a day. Amazingly enough, the old
man had treated his grandkids with far more respect
than he ever had his own sons when they were growing up—maybe he'd learned something from his
past mistakes, Bart hoped—and so both Daniel and
Lainey had always looked forward to their visits to
the Curly-Q.

Good thing, or Bart never would have agreed to
the deal.

"Daniel, Lainey—how about getting your bags."

"Right," his son groused, shuffling back toward
the vehicle, his daughter silently following.

Most of their things were already there—Bart had
sent a truckload ahead and Felice had made certain
the kids' rooms were set up with familiar treasures
in hopes that they would adapt to the move more
easily. For a moment, he watched them, intent on
unloading the vehicle, shoving at each other in their
best, normal brother-sister fashion.

Suddenly, Lainey screeched as Daniel pulled back
and raised his arm, her camera in his hand.

"Hey, maybe it's time I learned to use this
thing," he taunted.

"Give that back, Daniel!" she yelled as the automatic camera whined and clicked several times.
"Stop that! You're wasting my film!"

"Maybe I'm creating art." Her brother's taunt
was followed by more whines and clicks.

"Da-a-ad!"

"Give your sister her camera, Daniel," Bart said quietly. "Now."

Daniel lowered his arm and a livid Lainey grabbed it from him. She gave the instrument a quick once-over, as if to make certain it was all right. Her hands trembled as they ran over the camera that had belonged to her mother. Bart wanted to cuff his son, who knew exactly how important that camera was to his little sister.

"That was my last roll, you moron!" Lainey yelled. "Now I can't take pictures of anything! I *hate* you! I hate this place!"

Bart's insides wrenching, knowing it was the camera she was really freaked out about even if she wouldn't say so, he promised, "I'll get you more film later, honey."

But Lainey wasn't talking to him or her brother. She grabbed what bags she could handle and stomped toward the house. Apparently unconcerned, Daniel buried his upper body in the back of the vehicle.

Sighing, Bart finally turned his full attention to Felice.

"Where is everyone?" He avoided asking about his brothers. "Curt...Laredo...Enrique?"

"All gone. The only one left from the old days is Moon-Eye and he's picking up supplies."

All gone.

All driven away.

No wonder his father had been so anxious to turn the ranch into a family corporation, Bart thought. Undoubtedly, he figured that way his sons couldn't walk out on him again.

"We've had a couple of hands come and go since spring," Felice was saying. "Only one stuck—Frank Ewing."

"That makes three of us, then, to run this place," Bart said, realizing how impossible that would be. "I'll have to hire a couple of cowboys right away. Unless Reed and Chance show. What are the odds there?"

"Your father seems convinced they will come home."

Home? Would his two half-brothers think of the Curly-Q that way when Bart himself had had such a difficult time doing so? Finally, he got to it. "So, how's Pa?"

The housekeeper avoided his eyes. "The same," she said stiffly.

That bad. Despite the fact that he and his father had never been close—at least not since he'd been a kid—Bart's gut constricted.

"I guess I'd better go tell him we're here."

"Mr. Emmett knows. He's resting and said he would see you later."

Bart swallowed hard and nodded. And only hoped he hadn't brought his kids to more grief.

THE TERRITORIAL-STYLE building stood a welcome relief—a thing of gracious beauty amidst the ruins of Silver Springs. And the clack of the brass knocker against the door brought a beautiful woman to open it.

Wiping her hands on her lace-edged apron, the woman asked, "Can I help you?"

She quickly smoothed loose strands of thick blond hair from her face and checked the twist at her nape as if to make sure all was secure. The rest of her was equally elegant, Josie noted, from her pearl earrings to her Italian leather pumps.

"Are you Alcina Dale?" Josie asked in a hesitant, soft voice.

"In person."

"I understand you rent rooms."

Entrenched on the porch, face half-hidden by the shadow of a Stetson from which spilled her tangled light brown, shoulder-length hair, Josie felt anything but elegant herself.

"This *is* the Springs Bed-and-Breakfast," Alcina agreed, eyeing the single, aging leather bag Josie had dropped on the porch.

Josie knew what she must be thinking. A typical guest of a place like this wouldn't wear jeans ripped at the knees and dusty, down-at-the-heel cowboy boots, or a stained denim jacket slipped over a white T-shirt. But the town didn't have a regular boarding house, which is what she'd been hoping to find. This was the best suggestion the guy at the gas station could come up with.

Suddenly she realized Alcina was staring at her waist, where an inscribed silver buckle proclaimed her initials to be *J-W*. Self-conscious under the close scrutiny, Josie brought a hand to her belt and quickly covered the engraving.

"The problem is...um, well...I'm looking for work."

Alcina sighed. "The seasonal tourist rush is over, and I really can't afford to pay for help."

"I—I thought maybe if you had a really small room, you might let me help you around here for my keep.... All I need is a place to sleep and some food until I get a job. Then I'll pay you with real money.''

The note of desperation in her own voice grated on Josie. Sighing, she glanced down the twisted road that made up Main Street. Nothing for her there. Only a handful of occupied storefronts waged war against abandoned buildings and rubble left behind fallen structures.

''You're thinking you'll find work in Silver Springs?'' Alcina murmured ruefully.

''It doesn't seem likely, does it? I've never seen a town still alive and so dead at the same time.''

''Decades ago, Silver Springs was thriving. That's when my daddy and his two partners discovered a new lode of silver in the abandoned mine…but then the lode ran out. The town hung on for a while as if it could breathe life back into itself. But over time, everything changed. Businesses got tired. People got tired. Silver Springs just up and died. So, honey, unless one of the ranches around here needs a day worker, I'm afraid there's nothing here for you.''

Having been nearly ready to plead for help, Josie firmly tightened her lips and nodded. Her eyes misted over as she stooped to lift her bag…and she winced because the movement hurt.

She noticed that Alcina had quickly glanced to the street behind her, no doubt looking for a vehicle. But she had no car and no money…no way of getting anywhere else but her thumb.

Sweeping a tangle of hair out of her face, Josie turned to go. Alcina stared, eyes wide. Josie knew she'd caught a look at the nasty bruise along the left side of her temple and cheek. She tried to hurry away then, before explanations were necessary, but the other woman put out a staying hand.

"Wait."

Shoulders pressed down by the burden of having nowhere to go, Josie hesitated without looking directly at Alcina. She hated needing help. Hated being pitied as if she were a kicked dog or something as equally pitiful.

"What's your name?" Alcina asked.

She softly replied, "Josie," as she put her free hand to her middle, fingers tracing those initials on the belt buckle. She thought quickly. "Josie... Wales...."

"Josie Wales—now where have I heard that name before?" Alcina mused, pulling her mouth as if thinking about it. "Are you originally from these parts?"

"No."

"Oh, well, it doesn't matter, does it?" As if unable to help herself, Alcina said all in a rush, "I do have a small room off the kitchen that I don't rent to tourists. Actually, it's my ironing room, but there is a single bed and a dresser—nothing fancy."

Josie snapped up her head. "I don't need fancy."

Relief poured through her, lightening her load. She blinked rapidly, stopping herself from outright crying.

Alcina rushed on. "And I guess the whole house *could* use a spring cleaning."

"Spring?" Josie started. "But it's fall...isn't it?" *Confusion. Again.*

Alcina said, "That it is, but it's hard to get good help in a ghost town at any time of the year."

"I'm willing to do anything you need."

"C'mon inside, then. I'll show you to your room, and after my guests finish their breakfast, I'll feed you and give you the grand tour. You look like you could use a little rest. Then maybe later you can walk over to the grocery store and pick up a few things for me."

"Anything! Thank you."

Alcina stepped back to let her in. And yet she appeared troubled, as if she worried that she might have reason to regret her simple human kindness.

The flesh at the back of Josie's neck prickled at the thought.

One last look out to the empty street reassuring her, she stepped inside and took a look around at the elegant Victorian decor, as, behind her, Alcina Dale firmly closed the door against the unknown.

FEELING A WHOLE LOT better on a full stomach and from a lie-down, and with the knowledge that she would have a roof over her head that night, Josie Wales set off for the small grocery store at the other end of Main Street.

Other end.

Three whole blocks, with only a handful of establishments lining the winding street cut through low hills open for business—café, law office, bar, whatnot, doctor's office, home-and-feed, church, grocery, gas station.

And in between sat skeletal buildings in various stages of decay—reminders of a more prosperous era, as were those railroad tracks that went nowhere but along the boarded-up stagecoach stop. The single-story building of volcanic rock had wooden porches traversing the entire length of each side.

Other rutted dirt roads on either side of Main Street led to a few dozen homes whose size, condition and state of occupancy varied, as well.

Just outside of Silver Springs, what was left of a row of miners' shacks stood testament to the town's origin—the old silver mine. Some were little more than stone foundations. As she'd hiked in from the highway, she couldn't help but notice a strange-looking couple—squatters?—scurrying about the area, setting out displays that appeared to be made of animal bones. Odd, but nothing to unsettle her.

Not much to Silver Springs, Josie thought, but something about the town drew her, made her think she might be safe here.

Safe. Was she?

Despite the warmth of the late October afternoon, a chill swept through her, suddenly making her feel as if hostile eyes followed her every movement. She glanced around. Two women were chatting outside the doctor's office across the street. A cowboy was hunkered on a bench outside the bar just ahead, his wide-brimmed hat bowed as if he were asleep. Behind her, an old junker of a car headed out of town. And at the end of the street, a fancy black SUV covered with red dust turned out of the gas station.

Nothing out of place…just like before, when the trucker had stopped his rig to let her out of the cab and she'd sworn someone was watching, though she hadn't caught anyone at it…and yet…

What was wrong with her? No one could be following her. No one even knew where she was.

It was just that she hadn't really felt safe since awakening in that hospital bed.

And now she was an outlaw on the run!

She glanced at the black SUV that crept along the street in her direction. The dark-haired driver seemed to be searching for something…or someone.

Her?

Muscles bunched, she was ready to bolt when he looked directly at her…through her…beyond her….

Realizing that she was of no interest to him, after all, Josie trembled with relief. Not that she could help being a bit paranoid. Undoubtedly that's what was making her feel those invisible eyes on her.

Bringing her forefinger to her belt buckle, she traced the initials again and again.

J.W.…J.W.…J.W.…

Josie Wales was as good a handle as any.

She had to calm down. Get herself straight. Make plans.

Stop imagining dangers where there were none.

Lost in thought, Josie at first ignored the faint sound coming from the abandoned building preceding the bar. But as she drew closer, she realized it was a cry of distress. Heart thumping, she slowed her step in the deep afternoon shadow cast by the structure and strained to hear.

A scrabble was followed by a sharp "Meow!"

A cat.

Relief shot through her. Just a stray animal.

But as she moved on, the cry grew pitiful, the scrabbling more frantic, and she stopped again as she drew even with the entrance.

"Mee-ooww!"

Josie closed her eyes and sighed. Undoubtedly she would be on a fool's errand, but she couldn't go on until she was certain the cat was all right.

The door hung crooked on its hinges and she had

to throw her shoulder into the wood to budge it. The panel inched inward, then twisted so that the top hinge gave. Levering the unexpected weight, she took a quick look around, but nothing had changed—women still talking, cowboy still sleeping, SUV still inching along.

''Great. Add destruction of property to my crimes,'' she muttered. ''Not to mention breaking and entering.''

Another cat cry set her in motion.

Break and enter she did, stopping for a moment to let her eyes adjust, the interior being lit only by the smidgen of gray allowed through the grimy front windows, and that extending only a few yards before fading to pitch black.

How thrilling! she thought wryly. She'd never been able to see well in the dark....

Where had that thought come from?

Josie shook away another chill and concentrated.

Rubble decorated the interior of the abandoned shop as far as she could see—what was left of counters and shelves littered with plaster and rotting chunks of wood. As she moved with care, the floor squeaked and bounced beneath her boots. Her stomach tightened.

The place was dangerous, rotting, collapsing in on itself!

Stopping, she took a deep breath.

If any place could inspire paranoid delusions, this was it. Danger could lurk in every dark corner...in every inch of the area that she couldn't see.

But of course it didn't.

The only danger here was what she could inflict on herself.

Even so, reluctant to continue without reconnoitering, Josie softly called, "Kitty, where are you?"

A creak to her right startled her into stepping that way.

Until a loud "Mee-oow!" pulled her in the opposite direction.

For a second, she went rigid. Sounds from two directions? Then giddiness bubbled through her. The rotting wood was protesting, it being disturbed, was all. She veered left, feeling all but swallowed by the dark.

"Kitty, you owe me big time."

She inched along until her foot hit something solid, the clank punctuated by a growl and a hiss.

Puzzled, she hunkered down. "Hey, I would never hurt you." And reached out blindly, expecting to ruffle some fur. Instead, her fingers met an unexpected resistance, cold and hard. "What the heck…?"

Leaning forward, she ran her hand along the solid object and murmured reassurances. The cat continued to growl with increasing urgency. The angry-frightened protest raised the hair on the back of her neck even as Josie realized the poor animal was trapped in a cat carrier.

Who would leave a caged cat in an abandoned building?

Instinct snapped her upward, but upon rising, she whacked her shoulder into something ungiving. She took a misstep and twisted her ankle.

"Aah!"

Arms flailing, Josie tried to catch herself. She imagined hands on her even as she took another blind step. Rough hands. Hands that pushed her so that her boot heel came down hard and shoved right through some rotted boards.

For a second she felt suspended...her world turned upside down...a roller-coaster ride...only this time with no safety net....

Chapter Two

Josie fought the panic attack that threatened to engulf her. Shaking…lack of breath…heart threatening to pound right out of her chest.

She hadn't fallen far, she told herself as rationally as she could—only to the rotting floor—but her boot had gone through the boards, ankle-deep. She tried to free herself. But no matter how she turned or twisted her foot, she couldn't seem to manage it.

She was stuck!

Gasping for air, ribs and chest hurting where the seat belt had constrained her, she told herself to calm down. She was all right. She could get through this.

Unless…

Ghost memories of hands on her, touching her, pushing her, jumped back at her in a flash.

But had it really even happened?

She couldn't say for certain. She only knew that same sensation of personal violation had invaded the deep unconscious from which she'd thought she would never awaken while in the hospital. That same sense of physical unease had pressed down on her then, too.

The same paranoia.

Josie willed herself to focus on any lurking danger, but she could no more see a threat in the dark than she could her own fingernails, which were digging painful little ditches in her palms.

Through fear-stiff lips she whispered, "Is someone there?"

Every muscle in her body tightened into knots as she waited for a response.

"Meow."

She jumped. The cat! She'd almost forgotten....

"Yes, kitty, I'm still here."

But was she the only one?

No noise alerted her to another presence. No sudden intake of breath. No stirring of foot against rubble. And the cat's call had once more sounded pitiful rather than angry.

If any threat *had* been present a moment ago, surely now it was gone.

Not wanting to think too deeply on it, she muttered, "Give me a minute, kitty, and I'll get us both out of here." And willed her hands to unclench.

Panic receding, Josie carefully slid her bottom forward over creaking boards and hunched up as close to her foot as her aching middle would allow. Blindly, she felt for the problem. Ragged wood had gashed and caught the worn leather of her boot and held it fast in several places.

Concentrating on working herself free, Josie almost missed the import of several quiet footfalls coming at her.

Then her hands stiffened again and sweat popped down her spine. A wave of intense heat poured through her as she literally ripped at the wooden slivers trapping her boot. Carefully, she wiggled her foot and pulled...even as a bright light suddenly blinded her more effectively than had the dark.

"What are you up to?" came an arrogant male demand.

Freed at last, avoiding looking directly into the beam, Josie put out a hand to shade her eyes. All she could fathom was a dark silhouette against the bright light. Her impression was of a tall man, one broader than most. She cautiously rose, careful not to step back into trouble.

"Maybe you should be the one answering that," she said more bravely than she was feeling.

"I'm not the one sneaking around here in the dark."

"I wasn't sneaking! I heard the cat—"

"What cat?" The disembodied voice sounded rife with suspicion.

Helpfully, the animal she'd been trying to rescue chose that moment to agree in the tiniest of voices—one Josie hadn't before heard—almost as if the feline were satisfied that her rescue was imminent.

The bright beam moved away from her toward the sound. She followed its course and finally was able to see the object she'd been fumbling over—a cat carrier with a glowing-eyed occupant peering out hopefully at them.

"Meow."

Josie reconnoitered, decided to get going and fast. But she wasn't about to leave the animal she'd determined to rescue. Thinking she could use the carrier as a weapon if she needed to—only if forced, of course, lest she further scared the poor creature inside—Josie swooped down on the cage. Ignoring the pain that twinged through her middle, she grabbed hold of the handle and proceeded to bluff her way out of the place, a distant gray haze identifying the general area that would lead to the street.

"Wait a minute!"

She quickened her step toward the film of light ahead, muttering, "Forget it. I'm outta here!"

The beam turned and swept before her. "Have some light before you really hurt yourself."

Josie didn't so much as falter. She kept right on going, straight out the door. Just in case she needed some, she looked around for help. The street was deserted—no chatty women, no sleepy cowpoke. But the black SUV had been abandoned at the curb opposite.

Had the driver been looking for her, after all?

Knowing she was alone but for her furry companion, Josie flipped around and bravely faced him.

He *was* tall. He *was* broad. And he was definitely unhappy. A scowl marred an otherwise attractive face—rather, as much as she could see of it beneath his broad-brimmed black hat. His hard gaze met hers, trapping her as effectively as had the broken boards.

Any thanks for the rescue she might have uttered died on her lips.

"So what was this cat doing inside what should be a boarded-up building?"

His demand for an explanation immediately made her bristle. "Like I should know?"

"You obviously knew the cat was there."

He moved closer to her, and his aura of power threatened to smother her. Normally she didn't put credence to that sort of thing, but when her pulse lurched, Josie took a step back. Then she winced when the cat carrier smacked into a sore spot. A sudden acid taste in her mouth soured her mood further. If anyone had meant her harm in there, this man couldn't have been the one, she assured herself, or he wouldn't be asking so many questions.

Realizing that she probably had been alone, that she had spooked herself, and that her imagination had conjured some other "presence," that, sensing her fear, the cat had appropriately responded to, Josie couldn't figure out why this stranger had such a suffocating effect on her.

What in the world was wrong with her?

"I told you I *heard* the cat," she finally said to break his invisible grip.

"And so you just went inside…"

"Right."

"…and wandered around a decaying building blindly."

"Why should I explain myself to you, anyhow?"

She tried pushing by him, but he caught her upper arm and held her fast. And though he didn't hurt her, his fingers seemed to burn into her flesh right through the denim jacket. Her heart at first fluttered, then began to pound.

"We're not done here."

She went still and cold inside, and with difficulty, choked out, "What are you? A cop or something?"

The thought made her fight panic once more, if for a very different reason. What if there *was* a warrant for her arrest? What if he really *had* been searching for her?

His "Not exactly" didn't exactly relieve her building anxiety.

"Then you won't mind if I get going." Pointedly,

she stared at his hand on her arm until he let go. Her tense stomach relaxed and she trembled with relief.

"Where to?"

"Home."

"You live in Silver Springs?"

Of course he would know everyone who lived in a town this small. "Well, I do for the moment... over at the Springs Bed-and-Breakfast."

He seemed to digest that before musing, "The bed-and-breakfast, huh? Then what about the cat?"

Josie stared at him stupidly for a moment before it dawned on her. "Oh, right."

She couldn't just surprise the woman who'd been good enough to give her shelter with another mouth to feed...possibly an unappreciated mouth. Besides, the cat probably had an owner somewhere looking for her.

She raised the carrier and stared at the little white face edged by soft gray ears and a gray chin. Almond-shaped blue eyes stared back at her trustingly.

Josie asked, "You don't happen to recognize her, do you?"

"Her?"

"The cat. Just a guess about the 'her' part," she added hurriedly.

"Afraid not."

"Maybe she knows how to get herself home."

Not knowing what else to do, Josie set down the carrier and opened the door, all the while praying the owner would be glad to see the animal. Heaven forbid some irresponsible person had been trying to get rid of a pet...exactly what she feared, considering the circumstances.

But when the cat stepped out of her cage, she didn't run off as Josie had expected. Instead, the animal pranced, showing off her beautiful white-and-gray coat, then arched her back and rubbed herself against Josie's legs.

"She likes you."

Caught by the man's obvious amusement, Josie whipped up her head and frowned. "She just likes being out of the dark." And *she* liked it better when he was being hostile.

"More than that," he murmured, as the cat suddenly made a demanding sound and leaped straight up.

Instinctively, Josie caught the cat, who immediately settled in her arms, purring as though she was where she belonged.

"Oh, great, what do I do now?" she murmured.

When she glanced up, the man was watching her intently, his expression strange. For a moment, she was caught. Mesmerized by a pair of the bluest eyes she'd ever seen. High cheekbones and a well-defined jawline gave his face an edge that only the slight cleft in his chin softened. Mouth dry, she stared back, vaguely aware that she was holding her breath.

"Meow!" the attention-deprived cat protested, jolting Josie into sucking in some much-needed air.

"So what *are* you going to do?" the man asked. "With the cat?"

"It doesn't look like I have a choice at the moment, does it? I'll have to take her with me." Josie scratched the creature's head and ran her fingers over the silky ears. "Don't worry, Miss Kitty, we'll figure out something until I can find your owner."

And figure out how to feed the poor creature. "How are you at catching mice?"

The cat purred in answer.

"Doesn't look like any mouser to me," the man said, again seeming amused. Then he echoed, "Miss Kitty?"

"As good a name as any."

"*You* wouldn't have one, would you? A name, that is?"

"Josie Wales," she said, this time without hesitation.

No harm in giving him a name that wasn't even hers. The initials were right. She'd grabbed at the first thing that came to her mind. Still, she looked away from him and busied herself shushing Miss Kitty back into her carrier.

"Josie Wales?" He seemed about ready to challenge her, then said, "I'm Bart Quarrels over from the Curly-Q."

Figuring the Curly-Q must be a local ranch, she nodded, lifted the occupied carrier once more and said, "I'd better be on my way, then."

"Guess you'd better. I could give you a ride."

"Not necessary. I like walking." But a niggling at her conscience kept her from starting right off. "Hey, uh, Bart...Miss Kitty and I thank you for the rescue even if we didn't need one."

"I live to serve," Bart said dryly.

Grinning despite herself, Josie set off, wondering how she was going to explain the cat to Alcina— not to mention the lack of those groceries she'd set out for.

BART WATCHED JOSIE WALES rush down the street, cat carrier in hand. Something odd about the woman.

He couldn't quite pin it down, but something was definitely off.

Had she been afraid of him simply because he'd given her a scare? Instinct and more than a dozen years in law enforcement told him there was more.

Having filled his gas tank and bought half a dozen rolls of film for Lainey, he'd merely been taking a good look around before going back to the Curly-Q when he'd spotted Josie walking down the street.

She'd seemed...furtive. He couldn't describe her demeanor any other way.

Cop instincts kicking in, he'd watched her. And when she'd disappeared into the abandoned building, he'd naturally followed to see exactly what she'd been up to. Not that it was any of his business in the first place, he reminded himself as he climbed into the four-by-four.

He had to shake away her vulnerable yet spunky image. He had no business prying into her life any more than she had business in his. He'd turned in his deputy's badge—at least figuratively—to work the Curly-Q. And he'd better get back to the ranch and his kids—as far as Bart was concerned, his only responsibilities in the foreseeable future.

EMMETT QUARRELS grinned to himself as he listened to the house come alive around him. *Thunking* footsteps...raised voices...blasting music, if a body could call it that. Sweet, sweet sounds.

For too many years, it had been just him rattling around these rooms until he was nigh sick unto death of his own miserable company. If not for Felice, he would long ago have gone stark, raving mad. But Felice, as fond as he was of her, wasn't family.

And if he hadn't done something drastic, he might never have seen his grandkids again, now that their mother was gone. Sara, Bart's late wife, had always done right by him—he'd say that for her.

His three boys had all abandoned him and the Curly-Q years ago like each of their mothers had before them, but he'd finally fixed that.

Not that he'd had a choice in the matter.

Now they would all come home like their mothers never had.

A soft knock at the door startled him out of his reclining chair, where he'd been reading his latest *Modern Rancher Magazine*.

"That you, Felice?"

"No, Pa, it's me, Bart."

Heart lurching, Emmett quickly dropped the magazine and slid onto the made four-poster bed, pulling the afghan Felice had crocheted for him last Christmas up to his waist.

"C'mon in, son."

The door swung open and in stepped his oldest. With his thick dark hair, deep blue eyes, and a six-foot-plus, muscular physique that only hinted at his real strength, Barton was the spitting image of Emmett himself when he'd been young. And, though his oldest would never admit it, they were a lot more alike than mere looks conveyed.

"Pa."

Those blue eyes were searching him far more closely than made Emmett comfortable. He pulled the afghan a little higher and mumbled, "You're looking fit, son."

"And you're looking better'n I expected."

"I have my good days as well as bad." Emmett coughed, the sound more of a wheeze than anything of substance. "Doc says I'm almost ready to get back to work…uh, nothing strenuous, of course."

As Barton stepped closer to the bed, his foot connected with the dropped magazine. It went scooting across the floor with a noisy flutter of pages. He bent over to retrieve it, and when he straightened, gaze connecting with the cover, his expression changed slightly.

He rolled the magazine and tapped it against his free hand as he moved even closer so he could stare directly down at his father. "I thought you were dying."

"Thought…or wished?"

"I didn't say that."

"Sounds like," Emmett grumbled. He couldn't remember the last time soft words had passed between them.

"Your legal eagle Howard Stiles said your health was preventing you from running the ranch," his son persisted. "And that you had a limited time left."

Maybe Barton *did* want him dead, Emmett thought with growing sadness. Then he and his brothers could have the ranch like he had promised…without the old man who'd made it what it once was…and who had obviously made them so miserable they refused to be around him unless there was something financial in it for them.

Had he been such a terrible parent?

Not wanting to think too hard on it, he muttered, "Seventy *is* a step closer to God than you are."

"You can't ever know about that for certain."

From the quick flash of pain crossing Barton's features, Emmett figured his son was thinking about the way his wife had been taken...and her barely half his own advanced age. Sometimes, life just wasn't fair.

"I'm sorry about Sara, son," Emmett said with a stiff sincerity he didn't often share. "I would've been at the funeral if I could've."

"You were sick that far back?" His son's gaze narrowed on him. "And you didn't say anything?"

Big troubles on the Curly-Q had kept Emmett from the funeral in Albuquerque, but again he hedged. "What? You think a heart gives out..." He snapped his fingers. "...just like that?" He'd kept the problems from his boys—figured they wouldn't willingly walk into a viper's pit—but they'd get the picture soon enough.

"No, of course not." But Barton's expression didn't grow any less suspicious.

"A man starts realizing he can't do what he used to, that he doesn't have the physical stamina he once had, and he figures the years are catching up to him, is all. But one day, he realizes that's just the tip of the iceberg," Emmett said ruefully. "That he's in serious trouble...trouble that he can't fix by himself..."

"Pa, exactly how long *have* you been failing?"

"Long enough I don't want to talk about it...if you don't mind."

Though Emmett could tell the boy *did* mind, he had the grace to back off. At least for now. Emmett figured it was a temporary reprieve, that Barton was merely holding his questions for later.

BART UNROLLED Pa's *Modern Rancher Magazine* and stared at the cover. Sick the old man might be, but he hadn't lost his interest in the thing he loved best—his spread. Not wanting that to be an insurmountable problem between them, he figured he'd better nip any problems in the bud right away.

"Listen, Pa, before I get the kids all settled in here for good, we gotta get something straight between us."

"What would that be?"

Locking his gaze with his father's in a nononsense way, he said, "That, from now on, *I'm* in charge."

In a too-obvious attempt to sidestep the issue, Emmett said, "Reed and Chance always looked up to you. They won't give you any trouble."

"It's not *them* I'm worried about."

Shifting under his son's stare, Emmett coughed again, this time with more intensity. Bart tried not to let his father's illness get to him. He had to be tough as nails or this wasn't going to work. He couldn't let Pa call the shots here. And it was in his nature to be suspicious of anything that seemed too good to be true.

Emmett said, "The fate of both the Curly-Q and Silver Springs rests on your shoulders, son."

"Silver Springs? Whoa! Stiles didn't say anything about that, Pa." Barton threw the magazine onto the nightstand that his father had built with his own two hands. "It's not part of the deal."

"The deal is to get the Curly-Q back on its feet and keep it that way. A healthy Silver Springs will be good for the ranch and vice-versa, especially since half of the property there is tied up in the family corporation papers. A town needs law and order, and you're the only one with any experience in that area.''

''We're talking about a ghost town, Pa!''

''One that never should've gone the way it did,'' Emmett muttered. ''It was a stagecoach stop on the Santa Fe Trail, for pity's sake! We can't abandon a piece of living history! If not for poor planning—''

''Try a changed economy!'' Bart cut in. ''A mine that closed down when it played out! A railroad that stopped running through the damn place!''

''But Tucker and me were men of vision,'' Emmett insisted, ''even if Noah couldn't hack it,'' he said of a third partner who Bart had never met. ''We should've found a way through the setbacks. Tucker might've given up and moved over to Taos, but not me. I've just been waiting for my chance…uh, a chance for us all, that is. I say it's not too late if the Quarrels men all pull together.''

Bart realized he'd been right. Even serious illness hadn't dampened his father's will. Pa was making plans like there was no tomorrow.

''Pa, you're stuck in some damn dream. When I was a kid, it was already too late! We'll be lucky if we can hang onto the Curly-Q and a way of life that's mostly gone now.''

But his father had never been able to accept defeat when he took a notion. ''More'n one way to skin a cat,'' Emmett grumbled. ''It seems tourists *like* visiting Silver Springs. Tourists have money burning holes in their pockets. And some people actually have been moving in, trying to make a go of it. Population in the town proper is more'n seventy now…give or take a body.''

"*Seventy?* And you think I should—what?"

"You're a lawman! Do what a lawman is supposed to do. Protect its citizens. Turn Silver Springs into a shiny town that'll attract new families. Grow it back to what it once was, for God's sake!"

Good Lord, the old man was deluded!

"I turned in my badge, Pa. I gave up work I loved to run this ranch, remember?"

Emmett slid his eyes away. "Yeah, yeah, I remember. But part of you will always be a lawman, badge or no badge. Can't take that out of a man. Besides, I figure you're gonna have lots of help around here, so you can whip Silver Springs back into shape in your spare time."

As much as the idea appealed to him, Bart recognized a pipe dream when he heard one.

"This ranch will take every drop of sweat I've got. Reed'll put his back into the place, but he's not a leader. As for Chance, he's not much of a worker, as I recall." Suspicions rising once more, Bart narrowed his gaze and glared at his father. "Unless you mean something else."

Emmett said, "All I meant is if you three boys all pull together, you can do anything." He put his hand to his chest and sighed. "Arguing knocks the stuffing outta me these days. I need my rest now."

Exasperated, Bart backed off. "All right. We can finish this later."

"Since you have time on your hands," Emmett suggested, "why don't you check on Silver Springs this afternoon personally and see what you think."

"Already did that. Wasn't impressed."

"Then look up Alcina Dale and hear what *she* has to say. Might change your mind."

"Alcina?" Barton appeared surprised. "Haven't seen her in nearly twenty years."

"That girl restored the old family home on her own," Emmett said, "turned that spook place into one of them fancy bed-and-breakfasts that tourists like so much."

"Bed-and-breakfast?" Bart echoed. He'd seen the place, all prettied up, on his way through town. "Not the Springs Bed-and-Breakfast?"

"How many do you think a town like Silver Springs could handle? Of course that's the one!"

Mulling over that information, Bart said, "Hmm, maybe she does know something I don't. I suppose it wouldn't hurt anything to talk to her."

"Good. You could do worse than a beautiful, smart, ambitious woman—even if Alcina is that reprobate Tucker's daughter."

"Pa, whoa."

Was Pa now trying to manage his love life? Bart wondered, not exactly ready for one, even though Sara had been dead long enough that he missed a woman's company. But his family took up all the emotion he had in him.

His family...that included his father.

"Pa," Bart said, a knot of worry making him ask, "you are okay, aren't you?"

Emmett stared at a crack in the adobe wall that needed fixing. "As well as can be expected."

Bart swallowed hard. "Can I tell the kids they'll get to see you at the supper table?"

"If I'm up to it. It's been a long time since we've had a family dinner in this house."

"I'll let you get your rest, then," Bart said, opening the door. "And, Pa..."

"Yeah, son?"

Bart shifted his piercing gaze from his father's face to the foot of the bed. "You might be more comfortable *resting...without your boots.*"

Chapter Three

Bart Quarrels was the last person Josie expected to find planted on the front porch of the bed-and-breakfast when she opened the door later that afternoon. But there he was, bigger than life, all but blocking out what was left of the waning sun.

"You!" she said.

"You!" he echoed. "Long time, huh?"

To be truthful, he didn't seem at all surprised. And why should he, Josie thought—she'd told him where she was staying, so he'd known exactly where to find her.

"It's been all of several hours," she muttered.

Her mind raced as fast as her pulse. What was he doing there? What did he want? The way his gaze seemed to pierce right through her... Her stomach churned, leaving a faint taste of acid in her mouth. Somehow, she convinced herself to calm down as a simple reason for his seeking her out occurred to her.

Her knuckles white on the door where she clung to it, she said hopefully, "So you what...played detective and tracked down Miss Kitty's owner?"

He shook his head. "Sorry. I'm here on another

matter altogether.'' But before she could panic, he added, ''Could you tell Alcina I'm here?''

''Oh.'' Then this didn't have anything to do with *her,* after all. Feeling foolish, Josie took a deep breath. ''She's not here at the moment. She headed over to the store.''

Alcina had decided to do the shopping herself, especially since getting supplies for the cat—including litter—meant taking the car.

''I can wait,'' Bart said.

While Josie wished she could find some excuse to refuse him, Alcina undoubtedly wouldn't like that.

''Well, c'mon in, then.''

She backed off and gave him extra room to enter. But Bart Quarrels didn't have to touch her to make her aware of him. All he had to do was show up, Josie thought, not liking the uncomfortable fact one little bit. And when he removed his Stetson, she liked her reaction even less. Had to clench her jaw to keep from gaping.

The man was more ruggedly attractive than she'd realized, if that was possible. Thick, nearly black hair spilled over a high forehead. And while she'd noticed the blue of his eyes before—how could she not when they'd seemed determined to split her in two and reveal all her secrets—she'd missed just how thick and long his eyelashes were.

Realizing she was staring and that, if his raised eyebrows were any indication, he was reading her mind, Josie felt heat creep up her neck.

''Uh, you can have a seat here in the front parlor, if you like,'' she said far too breathlessly. She wanted to kick herself. Really. Closing the door, she shouldered past him where he'd stopped as if to block her. "I need to get back to the kitchen."

"If you don't mind, I'll keep you company."

She did mind. Wishing she could ditch him, a self-conscious Josie led the way. She wasn't comfortable with Bart following her…sizing her up…drawing whatever conclusions that were whirling around in that hard head of his. She distrusted the too-easy connection she felt between them. Had to keep in mind why she was there.

Above all, had to protect herself.

Once in the kitchen, she took up where she'd left off applying lemon oil to the unstained pine cabinets that gave the already large room an airy feel she enjoyed, while Bart made himself comfortable on a nearby stool.

Alcina had merely asked her to tidy up and wipe down the tile counters and appliances—all of which had already been spotless. Josie wasn't about to be a charity case. She meant to earn her keep as she'd promised until she could find a paying job. And Alcina really could use her help to make the house shine—doing more than the necessities around a place this big was too much for one person.

His back to the breakfast bar, Bart watched her work. "So the cat is still here?" He was looking around as if searching for her.

"Until Alcina comes back with a pan and litter, Miss Kitty is restricted to the outside. I put her in the former chicken coop to give her lots of room. And boundaries. I wouldn't want her to wander off."

"She seemed too smart for that. I'd bet she knows a good deal when she lands in one."

"She did get some tuna for lunch," Josie admitted. "Alcina has a real soft heart for strays." Including herself, she thought thankfully.

"Actually, I was talking about you. That cat took to you as if you wore her brand."

Josie chuckled. "Yeah, she is a friendly little thing. Real sweet, too. You can't touch her without setting off her motor. And she makes these funny sounds as if she's talking to me."

"Odd that someone threw away such a nice cat."

A fact that had been bothering her. Why would anyone ditch a sweetheart of a pet? About to apply more lemon oil, she paused as the threatening sounds the cat had made in the abandoned building echoed in her head.

"Especially without letting her out of the carrier," Bart continued, distracting her from that line of thought. "Poor thing could have starved to death unless the owner meant to come back for her."

That gave Josie pause. "Oh, no. What if the owner does come back for her and she's not there? Maybe I ought to put up a sign...."

"Wouldn't hurt."

"Unless it wasn't the owner, at all," she added, her mind churning with the possibilities. "Maybe someone was playing a mean trick. There are some real nasty people in this world. They take pleasure in causing heartache and pain."

Something she knew deep in her soul.

"And then there are people like you," Bart said in a smooth, low voice that made the hair on the backs of her arms crackle. "So, Josie Wales, how long have *you* been lost?"

She whipped around to face him. "Lost?"

"Here. In Silver Springs."

What a weird way to put it, though. "Not long," she hedged, wondering if this was idle curiosity or if he had a deeper motive for wanting to know.

"And you hail from?"

"Not around here."

"So...,will someone be looking for *you* to bring you home?"

"No one owns another human being!" she snapped, heart pounding with the possible implications.

Bart fell silent at her overreaction, but Josie felt his unspoken questions all the same. They were there in the way he looked at her, as if she were a puzzle he was trying to put together.

Finally, he said, "I just meant your family might be missing you some."

"I don't *have* family."

The words blurted out of her mouth before Josie even knew she would say them. They came to her quickly and naturally...a truth that inexplicably saddened her.

"You mean a young thing like you is all alone in this world?"

"Thirty-two is not all that young," she informed him.

Again, speaking without thinking, Josie realized, a little startled by the way she automatically responded to Bart's baiting. She was getting that feeling again—the one that put up her back at what on the surface were innocent questions, when they weren't anything of the kind.

He was digging, but for what? Had he even come

here to see Alcina, or had that been a convenient story?

Having finished applying the lemon oil, she took a clean, soft cloth and, starting with the end of the kitchen as far as she could get from him, began rubbing the film of lubricant into the wood.

And all the while, she was aware of Bart Quarrels watching her…wondering…making her want to run and hide from him.

"So how do you know Alcina?" he asked next.

"I don't. I just have a room here."

"That why you're cleaning the kitchen?"

"Right." She concentrated on the next cabinet. "For the time being, I'm working for her." Then, tired of the cat-and-mouse game, she set down the rag and faced him directly. "How many more questions are you planning to ask me, anyway?"

They stared at each other and she could almost see the little wheels spinning in his head. His eyes narrowed and his features drew into a bemused expression. Before he could come up with an answer, however, the door off the mudroom swung open.

"I'm back!" Alcina called.

Reprieve!

Without a by-your-leave, a relieved Josie turned her back on Bart and hurried out of the kitchen. Instant relief the moment she left his presence!

"Here, Alcina, let me take those. You have a…uh, gentleman caller."

"Really." Alcina's pale eyebrows shot upward. She turned over the sacks of groceries, saying, "Then I guess you'll have to wait for the cat litter."

"If it's still in the trunk, I can get it."

"It's awfully heavy—"

"I can get it," Josie firmly repeated.

"Well, if you're sure." Alcina handed over the keys, then stepped into the kitchen where she made a sound of pure pleasure. "Bart? Is that really you, Barton Quarrels?"

"In the flesh."

Josie couldn't help but follow. She stepped back inside just as Alcina rushed over and gave the man a warm hug. Inexplicably bothered by the way he responded, with a quick grin and arms snaking around the other woman's waist, Josie whomped the sacks of groceries to the counter and swept back outside to get the litter.

The moment she stepped onto the back stoop, Miss Kitty rushed to her chicken-wire fence several yards away and protested the recent inattention.

"It won't be long now," Josie promised, stooping to stick her fingers through the wires and scratch a kitty ear. "Though you can't have the run of the house. Just the mudroom and the ironing room. We'll have to share that. But don't worry, I'll give you plenty of attention. You can even sleep with me if you want."

She thought she'd like that—having the cat's warm little body to cling to throughout the night. She took comfort in the thought that she wouldn't have to be alone, at least not for now.

Unbidden came another image of her with a much larger, human companion, limbs tangled together...

Shivering she opened the trunk. The twenty-five-pound bag of litter inside would last one little cat a month.

"Alcina must expect you to be around for a while, Miss Kitty."

Which made her feel a bit better about the situation, just in case she wasn't able to find the cat's real owner right away.

Still hurting, she carefully hefted the large bag of litter. A familiar weight, she thought, handling it easily once she straightened. It was mostly her side that bothered her when she lifted anything more than a few pounds. But she certainly wasn't helpless. Closing the trunk, Josie thought about putting up some Found Cat signs around town. She could make a bunch that night, then tomorrow morning do double duty. Post signs and look for a job. If that suited Alcina, of course.

Josie stepped back into the mudroom, expecting to hear Alcina and Bart in the kitchen talking together like...what? Old friends? Lovers?

Why the second possibility should bother her, she couldn't imagine.

Thinking she would remain in Silver Springs only long enough to get some folding money in her pocket and an idea of just how far it would take her, she muttered under her breath, "Makes no never mind to me."

Not that there was anyone to hear. The kitchen was empty.

Good. She didn't need any complications. Had no use for them. Especially not when a certain complication seemed bent on knowing more about her than she did about herself.

Even so, she was a bit disappointed to find that Alcina had moved her "gentleman caller" to the parlor. She could hear their laughter ring out from the other room.

She couldn't help herself. After fixing up the litter

pan in the mudroom, she moved to the door that led to the dining room, which led to the parlor. Holding her breath, she leaned into the wooden panel ever so slightly—cracking it open just enough to get an earful.

"So what do you know about her?" Bart was asking.

"Just that she needed a roof over her head."

Good Lord, they were discussing *her*. Maybe she *had* been the reason he'd invaded Alcina's home.

"Are you always so blindly trusting?"

A beat of silence was followed by Alcina's asking, "Do you know something I should, *Deputy* Quarrels?"

Pulse thundering, Josie backed off into the kitchen as he said, "It's just that I'd keep my eyes wide open if I were you."

Deputy!

So Bart Quarrels *was* the law...she'd been right, then. But he obviously didn't know about her or he wouldn't be sniffing around, asking all these questions. If he had facts, he would have arrested her by now. Obviously he had his suspicions. Instinct made her want to run again.

But run to where?

She had no one to run to...no place to go...no money to get her there.

And why should she leave this safe haven? Bart didn't know anything for sure. What she needed to do was to find a way to defuse him.

Clenching her jaw, Josie started unloading the supplies. She was in the middle of trying to figure out how exactly to do that when the kitchen door swung open.

"Josie, would you mind making some tea? Earl Grey, I think. And you'd better brew it strong. I can't imagine Bart drinking it any other way."

"Sure, Alcina," she said, thinking she couldn't imagine *Deputy Quarrels* liking tea at all. She figured the lawman would consider it a sissy drink. Then, again, perhaps he'd take anything Alcina cared to offer.

"And afterward, could you check on the Raton Room—that's one of those two smaller guest rooms in back that has the shared bath."

"I remember."

Josie had noted that Alcina named all her rooms—two suites, two rooms with private baths and two with shared bath—after New Mexican towns. The fancier the room, the fancier the town it was named after.

"Could you air out the room, maybe fluff up the pillows and lay out a set of fresh towels?"

"Yeah, sure. I didn't realize you were expecting another guest."

"I wasn't. I met him at the gas station, actually. Tim Harrigan's his name. A stroke of luck that he was looking for a place to stay for a few days and I just happened to have a room available."

More than one, Josie knew. Only two couples were currently staying at the bed-and-breakfast, and one of them was checking out the next morning.

"I'll take care of everything, Alcina."

"Thanks."

When Alcina went back to the parlor, Josie realized their conversation had given her adrenaline a rest. She felt far more relaxed than she had a few minutes before. Filling the kettle gave her additional breathing room. She needed time to think was all...on how to allay Bart's suspicion of her before he stumbled onto the truth.

She could lie outright, of course. Tell him what he wanted to hear. Feed him false information. *If* she could get away with lying without revealing her hand. The only problem was that Josie suspected she was far better at evasion than lies, and she didn't seem to be doing too well in that direction to begin with.

The only option left to her was to charm the boots off the man. Maybe if she could loosen up...act more naturally around him...stop acting like someone had stuck a prickly pear under her saddle.

Saddle...she was riding a flaxen-maned sorrel past scores of people....

Josie blinked and the moment was gone. Where had that come from? she wondered, hard-pressed to shake off the weird feeling it gave her.

While the kettle was on the boil, Josie found the cabinet that held an assortment of teapots. Her gaze landed on one that had *charm* potential. She pulled it out and set it on the counter, then found a tray. By the time the kettle whistled, the tray was loaded. She filled the pot, then carried the tea tray into the parlor.

Alcina was saying, "My daddy isn't what he used to be, either—not that I would ever suggest as much to him. It's hard on us, isn't it? Our parents getting older."

"Older, but not necessarily wiser. At least not in Pa's case," Bart said as Josie set down the tray on the low table between them. "He doesn't know how to wave a white flag, I guess. And teaching him is gonna be an experience I'm sure I'll never forget. At least I hope I get that chance. He's as much as said he could go at any time.''

''What does his doctor say?''

''Haven't talked to the doc yet.''

His gaze settled on Josie, no doubt because she stood there, staring at him, a wave of empathy washing through her.

Trying to act naturally, she asked, ''Want me to pour the tea?''

''I can handle it from here,'' Alcina said.

Josie nodded but moved off slowly enough to see if Bart had any reaction to her choice of teapots—a fat white porcelain cat that resembled Miss Kitty. She thought she saw his lips twitch just a little at her joke. Probably as good as she was going to get. When his gaze slid to find her, she gave him a tepid smile—this charm thing didn't seem to come naturally to her—but his attention was quickly commandeered by Alcina.

''So when is it you expect your brothers to move back to the Curly-Q?'' she asked as she poured.

''Who knows if they'll show at all.''

''I can't imagine *Reed* staying away, considering the circumstances.''

The little hairs on her arms prickling again, Josie froze in her tracks. The way Alcina had said Bart's brother's name struck a definite chord in her....

''Part of me thinks you're right on that score. But the way Pa used to beat him down when he was working his butt off... I just don't know if he's got good enough reason to come back for more.''

''I would think partnership in a family corporation would be enough. Reed always loved that spread better than anyone—your daddy and you included! Unless he has long-term obligations elsewhere, of course," Alcina said pointedly.

"Don't know about any obligations. None to a wife or family if that's what you mean."

"*Really.*"

Really...?

Alcina Dale was obviously more interested in Bart's brother than in Bart himself, Josie realized as she returned to the kitchen.

Now, why did that lighten her step as she took the back stairs up to the second floor?

Maybe after she finished checking on the room, she'd figure out a way to implement her plan to charm the boots off the lawman.

Josie only hoped she wasn't tempting fate, somehow....

From the linen closet, she gathered a fresh set of towels, then opened the Raton Room. The room might be narrow with only a single bed, a dresser and a rocking chair, but it was mighty cheerful, what with three windows on two walls letting in so much light. As Alcina had requested, she made sure everything in the room was in order, including opening the windows to let in a cross breeze.

While she was rearranging one of the lace curtains, a fancy new red truck pulled around the building and parked. She gazed down at the tall, fair-haired young man who alighted from the driver's seat and slapped a well-creased brimmed hat on his head. His jeans and denim jacket seemed equally worn.

Strange, but he didn't look the type to stay in a

bed-and-breakfast, Josie thought as he rounded the truck to grab a single bag from the back.

Then he hesitated and gave the building a long, serious stare.

Not wanting him to spot her, Josie instinctively jumped back from the window. It wouldn't do to let him think she was spying on him.

Not that she could tell exactly where he was looking through those sunglasses he wore. Even as she thought it, he removed them. But she was too far away to tell anything anyhow.

Suddenly the man jerked around as if startled and moved straight to the old chicken coop.

Josie moved in closer to the window and barely got a glimpse of Miss Kitty all fluffed out before the animal disappeared into the rickety building itself. The man hesitated only a second before turning back to the house.

Wondering what had irritated the cat this time, Josie took a last look around, left the bedroom and checked the bath. Everything in order. She hurried downstairs, expecting the new guest would be waiting for her to show him up. But from the sound of Alcina's voice and footsteps on the front staircase, she guessed he was being seen to.

Ready to try for charming, she swung open the door to the parlor. Empty. She was only marginally disappointed. Best-case scenario would be that *Deputy Quarrels* had already lost interest in her. Sighing at her reprieve, she bent over the table to remove the tea service.

A glance out the front window assured her that Bart was actually leaving. He was just opening the door to his SUV. She watched him hop inside in one fluid motion and imagined him mounting a horse with equal grace.

Shaking away the odd feeling that picture gave her, Josie immediately carted the tray into the kitchen and then headed outside to fetch the cat.

Chapter Four

Bart was still thinking about Josie Wales as he rounded up his kids for supper and herded them into the dining room. Felice had outdone herself, polishing the big pine table, the center of which was decorated with ivory candles of different thickness and heights, interlaced with dried flowers of the region. Five places had been set, so it looked like his father was going to join them for supper.

Both kids went for the same chair. Daniel won the struggle.

"Big jerk," Lainey muttered.

"Lainey, why don't you sit here," Bart suggested, indicating the end chair that was usually his. "And I'll sit between the two of you."

"I'm going to help Felice," his daughter said, already flouncing toward the kitchen.

Bart looked at his son. "Could you possibly go easy on your sister for a while? You can see what a hard time she's having, can't you?"

Daniel mumbled, "Yeah, sure," and looked away.

Leaving Bart to think about Josie some more. That woman had a way about her that inspired his interest, the real reason he'd taken his father's suggestion to look up Alcina. Not that he hadn't been glad to see his old friend, as well. Of an age, he and Alcina had gone through both grammar and high school together. At one time, he'd suspected Pa and Tucker Dale had more permanent plans for the two of them, but he'd never been drawn to Alcina in that way, nor she to him. He'd seen her more as the sister he'd never had, not like...

He'd almost thought her name, Bart realized.

Josie Wales.

But, no, that was wrong. He wasn't attracted to her. His curiosity was piqued, was all. A stranger in a ghost town, getting herself all tangled up in rescuing a discarded cat was an oddity in itself. Plus that stranger had been hurt—he'd seen it both in her face and in the way she'd had trouble moving. But when that stranger played mysterious, as well, not willing to give over one detail of her background, he couldn't help but wonder...

He should mind his own business, he knew, but it was hard shutting off the lawman part of him, badge or no badge. His father had been right about that.

Coming back into the room with a dish of pinto beans and a basket of rolls she set on the table, Lainey frowned. ''I thought Grandpa was eating with us.''

''Would I miss a meal with my favorite granddaughter?''

Bart spun toward his father, who'd arrived on cue. Pausing in the doorway, practically beaming, Emmett Quarrels looked thinner, less robust than he had the last time Bart had laid eyes on him. And yet he also looked like a man who was content rather than one who was dying.

Ignoring Bart's instructions about not goading his sister, Daniel said, "You mean your *only* grand-daughter."

Bart couldn't miss the strange expression that crossed his father's face.

"Well." The old man wheezed a little as he entered the dining room. "Don't go getting all technical on me. I'm trying to say it does an old man's heart good to see his grandkids. I'm glad you're here. Both of you."

As he circled to his seat at the head of the table, he met Bart's gaze, and yet Bart didn't feel included in the warm welcome. His presence had been expected, although not necessarily appreciated. Big surprise. It really would kill the old man to express any kind of affection to one of his sons. He used to drone on about family loyalty. Love had never entered the discussion.

"Good. Everyone's here," Felice said as she brought in a platter of grilled skinless, boneless chicken breasts and assorted grilled vegetables.

"What's that stuff supposed to be?" Emmett demanded.

"Heart-healthy food." Felice gave him a challenging expression.

Emmett glared at her as he took his seat. "Next you'll be trying to feed me oatmeal for breakfast instead of bacon and eggs."

"Excellent idea, Mr. Emmett."

"Over my dead body!"

"Isn't that the possibility?" Felice asked.

Startled by Felice's unnaturally harsh comment,

Bart narrowed his gaze first on her as she set down the platter, then on his father. But both of them donned their players' faces. His kids couldn't hide their reactions quite so easily. Daniel was practically glowering, while Lainey appeared ready to burst into tears again.

"It looks good, Felice," Bart said, in an attempt to play peacemaker. "Anything you cook does. Sit."

"Of course, Mr. Bart," she said smoothly.

"Let's eat."

For the next few minutes, conversation was directed at passing food and filling drink glasses.

It had been years since Bart had partaken of a meal in this room. And yet it was all so familiar. The weathered *trastero* in the corner that held the same dinnerware he'd eaten off of as a kid. The long pine table along one wall that served as a buffet when the place got really crowded. Area rugs woven by Native Americans decades ago were still scattered over the planked floors. A chandelier made from an antique wagon wheel overhead. A real ranch dining room.

His ranch now. Or was it to be his and his brothers?

"So when do you expect Reed and Chance to arrive?" he asked his father.

"Not exactly sure."

Noticing how particular the old man suddenly seemed to be about his pinto beans—as if he had to choose them one at a time from the big bowl—Bart narrowed his gaze and asked, "They didn't give you a date?"

"Reed's the foreman on a ranch up in Colorado."

"I'm aware of that."

Bart had tried reaching Reed to no avail, however. He'd been too busy shipping cattle to return Bart's call. Or maybe he just hadn't wanted to talk to his big brother. No surprise there, either.

"Pa," Bart said, silently willing his father to be straight with him for once, "what exactly does that mean to us?"

"You know your brother. He has a sense of honor that won't let him leave until he sees the season through."

Aware that his father was being purposely vague, Bart pressed him. "So that means he'll be here...when? Next month? Before the holidays?"

"Probably then," Emmett agreed. He took a bite of the chicken. "Hey, Felice, this tastes better than it looks."

"Why, Mr. Emmett, that almost sounds like a compliment," she returned.

"*I* think it's all delicious," Lainey said.

"Me, too," Daniel chimed in.

"Sometimes it doesn't hurt to try something new," Emmett admitted, giving the kids a crafty expression. "Right?"

But Bart wasn't about to let his father off the hook so easily. "Whoa! We're talking business here. What about Chance?"

"Howard hasn't exactly been able to run him down yet."

"What?"

What had the lawyer been doing all these weeks? Chance couldn't be that hard to find. All Howard Stiles had to do was check every rodeo in the southwestern states. If Chance wasn't riding broncs, someone was bound to know where he was.

"Sounds like your lawyer isn't doing his job."

"He has a lead on Chance, so don't you worry."

"How can I *not* worry when this place is too big for one man to work?"

"Maybe you're familiar with the concept of neighboring."

Bart couldn't miss the familiar sarcasm his father aimed his way. "On sixty thousand acres? More than two thousand cows plus calves plus more than a hundred bulls. That's expecting a lot from people I don't even know anymore."

"Well, *I* know 'em. And there're four of us here if you include Moon-Eye and Frank."

Moon-Eye was getting up in years, not to mention the hired man wouldn't step one of his boots in a stirrup, so forget his actually riding a horse. His work was limited to chores around the buildings, and anything that could be done by truck. Cattle on the Curly-Q were still moved the traditional way— by men on horseback with the help of good cattle dogs. And Frank Ewing, whom Felice had mentioned earlier, was an unknown quantity as far as Bart was concerned.

"Four," Bart repeated, staring down his father. "Let's see—me and Moon-Eye and Frank make three if my math is any good. You weren't thinking about Daniel here, were you? 'Cause he's got to go to school, so any help he gives us is minimal— weekends only *if* his homework is done."

Emmett coughed. Or maybe he was just clearing his throat, Bart thought wryly.

"Well, I was kinda thinking *I* could do some of

the easy stuff,'' his father said. ''You know—drive a feed truck once in a while—''

''Not until I talk to your doctor.''

Silence.

Bart looked for the twitch in his father's jaw that was a tell-all and was rewarded with it in seconds. The old man's pot was stirred good.

''What do you need to talk to Doc Baxter about, anyway?'' he demanded.

''About *you*—what else? I doubt he's going to approve of a man with a failing heart doing anything more physical than turning on a television set.''

''I'm supposed to watch TV all day? Why don't you just take me out and finish me off now?''

''I thought the dinner table was reserved for more pleasant conversation,'' Felice interrupted, subtly tilting her head toward Lainey.

His daughter was gripping her fork, staring at her food, starting to close herself off again, no doubt at the mention of illness and possible death.

Feeling wretched, Bart tried to help the situation by bringing the conversation back to the ranch itself. ''Hey, Pa, driving around the ranch today, I noticed more than a few cows still have their calves with them.''

''Most do, actually,'' Emmett admitted. ''We've only got a few hundred head ready to ship out.''

''Pretty far behind schedule,'' Bart mused. ''The first order of business, then, will be to hire a few hands to get the job done right away.''

''You're going to separate the babies from their mamas?'' Lainey asked, seeming disbelieving.

''As soon as possible.''

''That's just cruel.''

"That's the way of the world, little girl," Emmett said. "The ranch world, anyhow. We run a cow-calf operation here. You know that."

"But why do you have to separate them?"

Emmett didn't hesitate. "To send them to another ranch that'll raise and fatten them up for market."

Lainey's face went so white her freckles seemed to pop. "That's horrible!"

"That's just the way of the world," he repeated, but this time, he didn't elaborate.

Lainey turned to Bart, her green eyes accusing once more. "I can't believe you'd do that, Dad!" she said, her voice rising even as she stood. Her slight body trembled all over. "Children should *never* be separated from their mothers!" She blinked and the tears started to roll. *"Never!"*

With that, she ran out of the room sobbing.

Daniel stood so quickly that he nearly knocked his chair to the floor. His face was a mask of pain as he mumbled, "I'll make sure she's okay," and then tore after his sister.

Heart heavy, Bart said, "I should be the one to talk to her."

But as he pushed back from the table, Felice said, "No, Mr. Bart. She needs her brother now, and I think he needs her, as well. You lost a wife, but they share the pain of losing a mother."

He understood that particular pain, if not so sharply, Bart thought, remembering how his own mother had died when he was even younger than Lainey.

When he was only a toddler, his father had managed to drive his tenderhearted mother away with sheer meanness. Or so he'd come to understand later. She'd divorced Emmett and had taken Bart with her from the Curly-Q to make a new life in Albuquerque with her parents. While Bart had been turned over to his father on occasion, his heart had never been in the visits, but he'd gone without a fuss so he wouldn't cause more trouble.

And then, when he was eleven, his mother had died of meningitis, of all things, having caught it at the local college where she'd been taking a class to better her chances at a good job. He couldn't remember her being sick a day of her life before that. She was hardly cold in her grave when Emmett Quarrels had come to claim him from his maternal grandparents. Against his will, Bart had been rounded up and driven back to the Curly-Q, where he'd gotten to know—if not exactly like—his two half-brothers.

Fight as they might, Daniel and Lainey were full-blooded siblings. They'd always been close. Daniel had alternately protected and tortured his little sister all her young life. They'd clung together through their mother's funeral. And it was only right that they continued to cling to each other and to support each other now. Bart didn't want to take that away from them.

"I don't know if this is going to work out," he muttered.

"It'll work out," Emmett said. "*You* worked out."

Bart didn't recall it quite that way. He just remembered being miserable. He hadn't been able to save one parent, hadn't been able to please the other.

And between him and his half-brothers, there'd been mostly jealousy and resentment, a love-hate relationship that was hard to define. Having chosen to stay on the ranch rather than live with his mother, Reed would have been the son in line to run it if Bart had never returned. But their father had made it clear that Bart was back to take that honor. And, in doing so, the old man had created a rift between the brothers. Not that the quiet Reed had ever put his resentment into words. As for Chance, his mother had run out on the old man and him—and the youngest Quarrels brother had done his best to make everyone else give up on him, as well.

Bart had always sworn things would be different for his kids, that he'd never put them through what his father had him. But lately—ever since making the decision to take on the Curly-Q and all it entailed—he'd done nothing but foster hostility and tears.

As if she knew exactly what he was thinking, Felice said, "Give them time, Mr. Bart. They're unhappy now, but they'll soon realize you have their best interests at heart. They'll come around, both of them."

Bart nodded.

They would have to come around, wouldn't they, or none of this was going to work.

FLAXEN MANE WHIPPING in her face, she felt as if her mount had wings....

Her heart soared and she gave herself over to the feeling of flying...faster...higher...scarier, for a dark figure stepped in their path.

She panicked and jerked on the reins. The sorrel flew upward now, hooves pounding the sky. Then they were off again, heading straight for the fig-

ure...a silhouette of a tall man wearing a brimmed hat...arm reaching out...hand grabbing at the reins.

The sorrel barreled around him to avoid his grasp.

The sudden movement made her dizzy. She clung on tight to the reins in one hand, the saddle horn in the other.

The very earth whirled around her and suddenly it wasn't a leather horn she was grasping...but a steering wheel...and she came to a thudding upside-down stop. Breath knocked out of her, she dangled like a puppet from a web.

Terrified, she cried out and thrashed to no avail...

Calming only when something soft and warm curled against her chest. Josie's eyes flew open to a dark that was still but for a low sound emanating from below her chin.

Purring...

Gasping, she remembered where she was and realized she'd been having a nightmare. Relieved that she had no reason for real fear, she snuggled in closer to the cat.

''Miss Kitty, I knew I could count on you,'' she whispered, even while wondering what man haunted her sleep.

Only Deputy Bart Quarrels came to mind.

Uncertain, though, she shifted in bed until her companion protested her lack of attention.

''Sorry.''

She cuddled the sweet animal who already seemed to belong to her. Not that she should get too attached, Josie reminded herself. She didn't know how long it would be before she had to leave this place in a heartbeat, just as she had the hospital the night before.

Before the authorities had even been informed that she'd regained consciousness, she'd crept away in the dark of night...had gotten to the high-way...had hitched a ride with a trucker who'd kept to himself.

Here was better, yet she hadn't really felt safe since awakening with no memory.

Oh, she could remember the things that didn't matter to her. Like who was running the coun-try...which television shows were most popu-lar...even what toy had been the bestseller the pre-vious Christmas.

What she couldn't remember were all the impor-tant things. How she'd landed in the hospital bed in the first place...why a sense of fear threatened to smother her at the oddest of times...or, most im-portant, who she was.

A woman with no name.

Would she always have to live a lie? she won-dered.

She'd come out of a deep, disturbing sleep that had held her in its hazy cotton trap for some time. While still half unconscious, she'd overheard strange voices talking about her, speculating about crimes that she might have committed. Those voices had said that the vehicle she'd wrecked had been stolen. That the police wanted to question her as soon as she was awake. That they were already run-ning the fingerprints found in the truck through the computer system.

Her fingerprints.

Josie rubbed the tips of her fingers against one

another—lightly callused, they spoke of hard work. She wondered if they really could reveal more, could really tell her who she was.

What crimes she had committed.

What kind of a person she was deep down inside.

She turned those fingers to the animal who trusted her so implicitly. Blindly, she searched for every sweet spot she could find to make the cat purr harder and louder.

Eventually, she allowed the vibration to seduce her back to a world where her real identity didn't matter.

MORNING CAME ALL TOO SOON. Still, Josie rose with a sense of purpose.

"I'm going to find you your real owner," she informed the cat, who watched her from the middle of the bed. "And me a paying job."

After showering, she wove her wet hair into a single braid and used makeup to camouflage the quickly fading facial bruise. She slipped into a fresh cotton shirt with long sleeves and a clean pair of jeans, then added the things she'd been wearing to the basket of Alcina's clothing that she'd left in the mudroom the night before. Even as she started the laundry, she smelled the fresh-brewed coffee and heard Alcina moving around, clattering pans.

Entering the kitchen, Josie grabbed a mug of coffee. Her plans to put up Found Cat signs and ask around town for work right after breakfast got Alcina's approval. Thinking maybe things would work out to everyone's satisfaction, Josie pitched in, making fresh orange juice.

"How long have you been on the road?" Alcina suddenly asked.

"Did Deputy Quarrels ask you to grill me?"

"Deputy...oh. I was teasing him. Bart's not a lawman anymore. He retired his badge to run his daddy's ranch. Actually it's the family ranch now, the biggest one around here. And like everything else around here, it's fallen on some hard times."

"He sure seemed like a lawman," Josie muttered.

"That's just Bart's way. He always did have to be on top of things."

Well, at least he wasn't officially on her case, though she suspected he would be—badge or no badge—if he got just an inkling of what she'd run from. Not wanting to encourage more questions she couldn't or didn't want to answer, Josie volunteered to set up the dining room.

Five guests were now registered at the bed-and-breakfast—two couples and Tim Harrigan, the lone man she'd seen arrive. He was the first to wander downstairs. Freshly showered and shaved, his light hair still damp, his pale blue eyes sparkling, he was easy to look at.

"Morning," he said cheerfully, looking her over with equal interest. "I'm Tim."

"Josie. Want some coffee?"

"You bet. Black'll be fine."

"Make yourself at home in the parlor if you want. Alcina's cooking up a storm. Breakfast will be ready in ten minutes or so."

"Great. I'm starving."

Back in the kitchen, she volunteered to help speed things along, but Alcina said she had everything under control and would call her when it was time to put the food on the table. Filling an insulated decanter with coffee, Josie brought it out to the buffet where she poured some into a mug for Tim, then joined him in the parlor.

"Thanks," he said, taking the steaming mug. "So, you like living here?"

"I haven't been in town long myself," she hedged. "Are you thinking of moving to Silver Springs?"

"Nah, probably not. I'm just kicking around for a while, and this town seemed like as good a place as any to spend a few days."

"You never know—it might grow on you."

"Never know," he echoed, saluting her with the coffee mug and gulping down half the contents. "You could help, tell me what sights to check out."

Josie laughed. "If there *are* sights, I don't really know about them yet."

He seemed hesitant, almost shy, when he said, "Maybe we could check them out together."

For some reason, the friendly suggestion made Josie uneasy. "I'm going to be looking for work."

He said, "No problem," but withdrew into his coffee.

Now feeling guilty, Josie silently blessed Alcina, who just then called her from the kitchen. "Sounds like breakfast is coming right up."

And the other guests were coming down the stairs. Two couples—one middle-aged, the other young and obviously newly in love.

For the next half hour, Josie kept busy serving food, keeping coffee mugs filled and setting the dirty dishes in the washer while Alcina ate with her guests.

They were all chattering like old friends, all except Tim, who was keeping to himself. He really *was* shy, Josie thought, almost sorry she'd turned down his friendly offer. And yet she had little interest in spending time alone with him. Or with any man, for that matter. Something about doing so frightened her.

Even as she thought it, a ruggedly handsome face came to mind. Josie pushed the lawman "who wasn't really" out of her thoughts and concentrated on doing a good job.

Once the dining room was put back to order and the laundry finished, Josie readied herself to job-hunt. She redid her hair, fixed her face, swiped on pale pink lipstick and grabbed the signs she'd drawn up about the cat. Leaving Miss Kitty in the chicken coop so the cat could get some fresh air and a change of scene, she set off.

Her plan was to check every business on one side of the winding street, then make her way back on the opposite side. Executing the simple plan didn't take long.

"Sorry, no work here" and "Ain't heard of no one looking for a missing cat" were typical of the responses she heard. Still, she did get permission to put up her signs.

When she arrived at the gas station at the far end of town, she got her first whiff of good news.

"Think they're looking for someone over at the bar," the owner told her.

Hope renewed, Josie set off, futilely checking with open businesses along the way to the Silver Slipper Saloon. The name was fancier than the place—a long room of dark wood and an oversize silver-framed Mexican mirror behind the massive bar. One end of the room was raised—a stage with electric footlights, though most of the bulbs were missing. And all around the room, walls were hung with aging posters of acts that had once appeared there.

Even though it wasn't quite noon, several men populated the place, mostly at small tables. The bartender was talking to a customer seated on a bar stool, but as she approached, nerves jumping, he turned her way, pale gray, nearly colorless eyes narrowing on her. Fortyish, he was a large man with rough features topped by a buzz cut that could be blond or silver—she couldn't quite tell in the low light.

"And what can I do for you?" he asked.

"I hear you're looking for help."

"Sorry, little lady, but I'm it," the man said. "Hired just last night. If it'll make you feel any better, though, drink's on me."

Her only hope gone, Josie figured nothing would make her feel better. But she was thirsty and could use a rest before heading back to the bed-and-breakfast.

She forced a smile. "Only if I can get a soda. Ginger ale?"

"Coming right up."

Josie slid onto a stool as he filled a glass.

He slid it to her. "Name's Hugh Ruskin."

"Josie."

"I'm sure glad you weren't around last night."

"Why?"

"A sweet-lookin' thing like you is bound to bring

in more customers—you would have had the edge on me."

"I don't know," Josie said, shifting uncomfortably as she seemed to do every time she was faced with a man paying her any mind. "You talk the talk."

He leaned over the bar and closer to her. Josie's fingers automatically tightened on her glass.

"I call 'em like I see 'em," he murmured. "And I sure would like to see more of you, little lady. How about here, tonight? Tab's on me and we can get better acquainted after the bar closes."

Again the odd feeling, stronger than her reaction to Tim Harrigan.

Smile a little stiffer, she said, "Thanks, but I'm not much of a bar girl."

"That why you were lookin' for a job here?"

"I need a paycheck. Period."

Not liking the surliness covered by Ruskin's smile, Josie drew back, thinking she'd better leave. But before she could make her move, the door behind her opened, drawing Ruskin's attention away from her.

"Welcome to the Silver Slipper!" he called out. "Name your brew."

"Coffee" came a familiar voice.

Josie sat frozen, keeping her back to Bart Quarrels as Ruskin got him his coffee.

"Here you go." He slid the mug across the bar. "We haven't met. I'm Hugh Ruskin."

"Bart Quarrels."

Of all the men to walk into the bar while she was there! Surely he wasn't following her.

"Listen up, men!" Bart said in a raised voice,

though the handful there could easily have heard a quieter tone. ''I'm spreading the word—we're looking for help over at the Curly-Q. Anyone here looking for work?''

''I got a friend who might be interested,'' one man said.

''Good. Tell him to come see me. I'm hiring right away. Anyone else know someone?''

Josie's heart thundered with the irony. Of all the people to have that work she sorely needed! She couldn't believe she'd ask *him* to hire her, but what else could she do? She'd checked every business in the town proper. If she ever wanted to get out of Silver Springs with folding money in her pocket...

She hesitated only a second before turning on her stool. ''*I'm* looking for work.''

As their gazes locked, Bart didn't try to hide his surprise. ''You, again.''

''Me,'' she agreed, her pulse once more threading strangely. The way he was staring at her...he might as well be touching her.

''Sorry, but I don't need a housekeeper or cook. I've got a big cattle operation to run and not enough hands.''

''What makes you think the only thing I can do is keep house or cook?''

He sized her up for a moment before asking, ''You have experience with cattle?''

A good question...one she couldn't answer.

Again the image of the flaxen-maned sorrel flashed through her mind.

''I have experience with horses,'' she said, somehow knowing that was the truth. How much experience, she wasn't certain, but she was desperate enough to bluff. Besides, she did have a set of spurs in her leather bag. That meant she did some serious riding. "If you have a big operation, you'll need a wrangler."

"I need someone who can do everything on a ranch. I need a real cowboy."

"And I am someone who can learn to do anything," she assured him. "Even be a cowboy."

She was crazy and she knew it. She was throwing herself in the lawman's path. Ex-lawman, she reminded herself. Besides, he was the only game in town, the only one who had the cash money she needed. Besides, she only had to work for him long enough to collect a paycheck or two.

Surely she could manage that and still escape him unscathed.

"Before you make up your mind," Josie said, a whole lot more calmly than she was feeling, "at least give me a chance to prove myself."

Chapter Five

No way did Bart want to fool himself into thinking Josie Wales was what he was looking for. It wasn't just that she was a woman, but that she was scrawny and secretive and a little bit desperate. But was the last really a bad thing? he asked himself, especially since help was harder to find than he'd counted on. Oh, he could get men eventually—send out the word far enough and a bunch of day workers with no prospects would come running.

In the end, he decided to relent, though why exactly he wasn't willing to say.

"If I do hire you," he told Josie, "you *will* have to prove yourself. And you'll be expected to do more than keep tabs on the horses."

"Just give me a chance to show you what I can do."

"This afternoon," he said decisively. Get it over in a hurry. Either she would do or she wouldn't. "You need directions?"

Josie grimaced. "What I need is a ride—no transportation of my own," she explained.

Bart could hardly believe her nerve. "Let's get

this straight. You want to work on my ranch, but you have no way of getting there yourself.''

Josie stared at him unwavering. ''Well, I *can* walk. How far is it?''

''Too far for you to have anything left in you by the time you get there.''

''Is this a deal-breaker?''

''We don't have a deal.''

''*Yet*,'' she qualified. ''I'm going to prove myself, remember?''

''We'll see.''

''Right, you will.''

She said it without hesitation, and from her very intensity, Bart sensed she would rather die than fail. He chalked up a couple of respect points in her favor.

''So how soon are we leaving?'' she asked.

''I need to make a few more stops. I'll pick you up at Alcina's in thirty minutes sharp.''

''I'll be ready.''

With that, she practically flew out of the place. Staring after her, Bart suddenly grew aware of curious eyes on *him*. He boldly met the nearest pair, which happened to belong to the bartender.

''You really going to make a cowboy of the little lady?'' Ruskin asked. ''Or you got *other* plans for her?''

Bart didn't like Ruskin's manner. He didn't like Ruskin. The man tried to put on a friendly tone that played false to Bart's sharp ears.

''What's your interest?'' Bart asked him.

''Curiosity good enough?''

''Sounds more personal than that.''

The bartender bared his teeth in a lascivious grin.

"I just wanted to make certain you weren't putting your own private brand on the little lady. I'm a man with an appetite, if you get my drift, and she certainly is one choice morsel."

Without thinking, Bart grabbed him by the shirt-front and pulled him off balance over the bar.

"Get *my* drift," he said, his face in Ruskin's. "No one talks about a lady like that while I'm around." Oddly enough, he took a personal affront since the lady in question happened to be Josie Wales.

Ruskin's spooky eyes narrowed on him, but the bartender didn't so much as twitch.

Silence.

Bart knew every customer was watching with unwavering interest to see what would happen next. But he wasn't about to provide this week's entertainment. He had too much else on his mind. He let go of Ruskin and dug into his pocket for his money clip.

Removing two singles, he threw them to the bar, saying, "Keep the change."

Then out he went, knowing he'd left behind an enemy that he didn't need.

ALCINA...

Josie had to tell her right away. The fly in the ointment, she thought. Here she'd let the generous woman believe she had an extra pair of hands around the bed-and-breakfast...well, she wouldn't disappoint Alcina. Maybe she couldn't manage breakfast—she was certain she'd have to be at the ranch at dawn—but she could always help with chores in the evening and on her day off. She wouldn't get paid for a week, anyway, so she still had to earn her keep.

Besides, she hadn't gotten the most positive of vibes from Bart. To cave in the way he had, he must be as desperate for help as she was for work. But she had no illusions about his keeping her if she didn't meet his standards.

The bed-and-breakfast might have her full attention, after all, she thought gloomily.

She found Alcina straightening the parlor and gave her a quick update. The woman seemed more than okay with the situation.

"I'm glad for you, Josie. I know you need work that has pay. Letting you stay in my ironing room for free until you're back on your feet isn't going to hurt me. As for working around here at night, don't be foolish. You won't have anything left in you."

Familiar words—Bart had said the same about her walking out to the ranch.

"I'll save some for you," Josie assured her. She might not be a big, strong man, but she was far from fragile.

"Let's wait and see," Alcina said cheerfully. She patted Josie's arm and headed for the kitchen.

It was only when the woman was out of the room that Josie realized Tim Harrigan had been on his way down, but he'd stopped halfway along the staircase as if he hadn't wanted to interrupt them. And yet he must have heard everything.

Descending, he confirmed the fact. "So you got that work you were looking for."

"On a trial basis."

He grinned. "I suspect you'll do all right."

If only she could deal with the owner...

"The Curly-Q needs more hands," she said, "if you're in the market for a job."

"Running cattle? Where's the appeal?"

"The paycheck at the end of the week."

He laughed. "Cowboy pay?"

Aware that *cowboy pay* wasn't much reward for long hours and physically tough work, she said, "It's more than I have in my pocket now."

Maybe Tim didn't need a job. From the looks of his shiny new truck—and considering he was renting a room here rather than in some cheap motel out on the highway—Josie figured he had a few bucks in his pocket.

The blare of a horn caught her attention. She glanced out the front window and saw the black SUV at the curb. Bart was already waiting. "My ride is here."

Tim gave her a smile and a thumbs-up sign. "Good luck."

"Thanks. I'll need it."

More to deal with Bart Quarrels himself than in doing the work he required, she was certain.

Josie ran out to the SUV and jumped into the passenger seat. On edge, she expected some comment meant to prick her, but without so much as a howdy-do, Bart took off. She waited for him to say something as they sped out of town, but he seemed comfortable in his silence…if she was not.

"Did you find yourself a real cowboy?" she asked.

"As a matter of fact I did—he's a friend of my youngest brother. He happened to be looking for Chance to get a lead on some day work in the area, so we both lucked out. He'll meet us at the Curly-Q later this afternoon.''

"How many hands are you hiring?''

"Depends. We already have two hands at the ranch. Only one of them is what you'd call a cowboy, though—I couldn't pay Moon-Eye enough to get him on a horse. If both my brothers show, I only need three hires.''

"One more, then.''

"At least.''

She didn't like the sound of that. Surely he meant to give her a fair shake. She bit back a direct response, though. She didn't need to get off on the wrong foot with him. The ranch itself was the safest topic. Besides, she wanted to know more about what she was getting into.

"How has your father been getting along with only two men on such a big spread?''

"He had more. Just couldn't keep 'em—the story of his life,'' Bart said, his voice tight. "The spread has suffered for it lately.''

Josie sensed big issues lay between Bart and his father. She figured it would be wise of her to stay clear of their personal business if she didn't want to irritate him. Besides, she didn't want him grilling her, either, and she guessed he would give tit for tat.

If the conversation got too personal, it would only be a matter of time before he figured her out. Even if he wasn't wearing a badge anymore, he was still a lawman. Couldn't take that out of a man like him.

"Tell me about the spread,'' she said. "It must be pretty big if you need—'' she quickly added up

the help he had and the help he wanted to hire
"—eight hands."

"Sixty thousand acres," Bart agreed. "We run a
cow-calf operation. Around two thousand cows and
a hundred bulls. I don't know how many calves we
have at this time. Pa said they'd only culled off a
few hundred so far, so our first big undertaking will
be to separate the rest from their mamas. You could
say we're a bit behind schedule."

Somehow, Josie gathered that before he said it.
She might not remember where she was from, but
no way was she a city girl. She absorbed the details
he offered about the Curly-Q as naturally as if she'd
lived on a ranch herself.

Which probably meant she had.

She closed her eyes in hopes of conjuring some
image that would prove it. But nothing came. She
fought the sick feeling that tried to get hold of her
every time she realized how truly lost she could get
inside her head.

That she could regain her memory at any time
was possible. The doctor had told her so in that short
time between her awakening and her escape.

She wanted her memory back...she needed
it...and oh, how she feared it.

That she had stolen the truck she'd been driving
when she had the accident was a dismal fact...and
yet one that she had difficulty accepting. Deep
down, theft—any kind of crime—was an anathema
to her, so maybe she wasn't a really bad person,
after all.

With all her heart, Josie wanted to believe that,
wanted to banish the guilt that lay below the surface,
threatening to swallow her whole.

Maybe she ought not think about anything but the present. She needed to keep her mind where it belonged. On her work. On the ranch.

And what a ranch the Curly-Q turned out to be. Acre upon acre of good-weather grazing land gave way to a bad-weather protective deep canyon, the very sight of which stole her breath away.

''It's beautiful.''

They'd only snaked halfway down the rock when she spotted a band of horses on the floor of the canyon. A couple of bays, an Appaloosa, a gray and a blue roan lined up along the road, waiting. When they hit bottom, the horses surrounded the vehicle, jogging on either side, acting as escorts to the buildings ahead.

The house was a sprawling adobe with wings that might have been add-ons to the original structure. The earth-colored walls were brightened by blue-trimmed windows and doors. As they passed the front of the house, she noted the long red chile *ristra* hanging from the door and, to one side of the stoop, the brightly painted ceramic pot large enough to hold a bluish-hued juniper bush.

''That building was our original barn, but now it's used for storage,'' Bart said of a long, dark red volcanic rock structure a hundred yards or so from the house. ''It also has quarters for our hired hand.'' He indicated another adobe a bit farther off. ''That's the bunkhouse over there.''

Two barking ranch dogs shot out of nowhere, joining the horses and adding the noise of frantic barking to the mix. Their mottled coats and cropped tails made Josie think they had Blue-Heeler in them.

Bart brought the vehicle to a stop in front of a

small pipe-and-wire-fenced corral alongside another building—a huge vaulted barn with an arched roof of corrugated metal.

As she stepped out of the vehicle, Josie looked around at their four-footed escorts, all still with them. Bart whistled to the dogs and gave them a hand signal. Both sat, though their tails continued to beat the dust and they whistled excitedly through their pointy noses.

"Meet A.C. and D.C.," he said. "Sisters out of the same litter."

Josie held out a relaxed hand so the dogs could get her scent. When they licked her fingers, she stroked each of their faces, murmuring, "Well, aren't you the friendly girls."

Then she approached the horse that had ventured closest—the blue roan, who was eyeing her with interest. "And what about you? Are you a friendly one, too?"

She kept her voice so low the horse had to prick its ears forward to hear, and she held out her hand much as she had to the dogs. When the mare snuffled her, she gently stroked its velvet nose, all the while keeping eye contact with her and talking low and sweet.

"You seem to have a way with Juniper there," Bart said. "She's barely green-broke. It'll take time and energy to make her into a good cattle horse."

"Don't worry, I'll manage it." Smiling, Josie carefully slid a hand around to the mare's neck and found a sweet spot. "We seem to have an understanding, don't we?" The other horses were eyeing her from various distances. "I only count five horses here."

"Don't worry, there're lots more where they came from," Bart assured her. "But these are the ones who've been ridden lately. Except for Juniper, of course. She's just been getting used to the place. Your first job will be to round up some of the horses from another pasture and bring them in closer to the barn. And then you'll have to ride each of them, see what kind of work they need. From what I understand, it's been quite a while since they've been ridden, so they're probably all full of beans by now."

A thrill of challenge shot through Josie and she prayed she could meet it. This would be her test, she knew. Rather, her *first* test. She didn't figure Bart for the type to go easy on her, ever.

The knowledge that she *could* do it—just as she knew she could make Juniper into a cattle horse—came as naturally to her as did her knowing what she preferred to eat for breakfast. Odd how this amnesia thing was so selective.

The other horses were determined to get in on the act now. They were pushing and shoving at one another for an introduction. Josie laughed and made certain each horse got a pat and a personal greeting.

Suddenly the feel of Bart's gaze pulled on her, drawing her attention from the equine reception.

Warmth flowed from her fingertips where they ruffled a mane, all the way down to her toes. He couldn't hide his approval and she couldn't still the excited thrum of her pulse. In some strange way, she felt as if she was home and couldn't say if it was him or the horses that did it for her. Most likely a combination. She'd sensed some kind of link with Bart right from the first.

It was an experience that left her breathless, and

restless, so that she was relieved when the dogs' barking again broke the connection.

A grizzled old man, average in height but square in stature, cut across the corral. The dogs scooted under the fence to dance around him. The man ignored them as he gave Josie the once-over with his good eye. It didn't take a genius to know this was the hand Bart had called Moon-Eye. His left eyelid was only half open and no iris was visible—only part of a milky white eyeball.

"Found yourself a cowboy, did ya?" he asked, tone skeptical.

"That's what we're gonna find out," Bart said. "Though it looks like a good beginning. Moon-Eye Hobb…Josie Wales. Moon-Eye has been a fixture on this ranch as long as I can remember. And as far as I know, he's never taken it upon himself to get on a horse."

"If God had wanted us to go gallivanting around on four legs, he would've given 'em to us."

Bart laughed. "He did in the way of horses. You just won't admit you think they're smarter than you."

"Ain't dumb enough to get on one, but they'd be dumb enough to let me," Moon-Eye protested. "I prefer my vehicles with wheels, if that's all right with you, son."

Despite their acerbic exchange, Josie sensed a genuine fondness between the two men.

"Frank's not back yet?" Bart asked.

"He's still out counting calves like you asked. Your kids went with him. Lainey had her camera."

"Sounds promising." To Josie, he said, "My kids are having some difficulty accepting the move."

Though startled by the mention of his having children, she said, "Moving is hard on anyone." She hadn't considered that Bart might be married... because, of course, she had no reason to care one way or the other. "Probably hardest on kids," she said of the moving, "because they don't have a say."

"I'm trying to do what's best for them. They haven't been the same since their mother died last year."

Died. He was a widower, then.

A rush of giddiness swept through her. Josie swallowed the smile that threatened her lips lest he think she was callous. What in the world was wrong with her?

"Losing a parent is difficult, but I'm sure they'll come along in time."

Losing *both* parents was even harder, Josie thought, somehow knowing that her own were gone. Not that she could remember the details.

"Enough about my personal life," Bart grumbled. "Let's take a pickup out to that horse pasture."

"You're coming along for the ride?"

"I wouldn't want you to get lost."

Josie was a little relieved that she wouldn't be left completely on her own as she'd expected.

"Got any cake we can bring along?" she asked.

She'd always thought the word *cake,* the nickname for protein pellets that reminded her of chunks of a cigar, as being odd. Then, again, horses usually went crazy for the stuff as if they were treats.

"Bribery, huh?" Bart asked.

"You object to my methods?"

"Not if they work."

Ten minutes later, they were cutting across an adjoining pasture in a truck nearly as old as she was. Josie was behind the wheel, Bart riding shotgun. Once he got her within sight of the band of horses, he let her take the lead.

She stopped the truck, got out and gave a series of sharp whistles. The horses' heads lifted and she repeated what she meant to be a command—that they pay attention and come to her. They began meandering her way, if with more curiosity than enthusiasm. That changed when she picked up the bucket of bribery from the back of the truck. She shook it so the pellets would bounce and make noise, all the while repeating the series of sharp whistles.

Then they couldn't jog fast enough.

More than a dozen horses crowded her, shoving at one another and her in the quest for treats. Josie shoved back and refused to let one of the big noses dip into the bucket. She made sure each and every horse took the cake directly out of her hand. They needed to make that direct connection, to know that she was their new boss.

"Okay, you lazybones, time to go to work." She threw the empty bucket onto the back of the pickup. Whistling again, she hopped inside, yelling "Yee-ha!"

Some of the horses appeared immediately on edge, prancing in place and nickering. Others turned their rumps to her as if to ignore her.

But Josie knew she actually had their undivided attention. She set the truck at a crawl and reached out the open window to beat on the roof with the flat of her hand. That spooked them into moving!

"Yee-ha!" she yelled again.

Some of the horses started to move off in the general direction of the barn. Others tried to wander away. She rode the truck the way she would a four-footed mount, circling and pushing the horses where she wanted them to go, all the while keeping up the encouraging noises.

Whistles…yells…pounding…

A few minutes later, the horses were streaming through the gate opening that put them right where she wanted them—in the smaller pasture next to the barn. She followed them through, then stopped the truck long enough for Bart to jump out and secure the gate.

As he slid back into the passenger's seat, he said, "Seems as if you know what you're doing."

Josie grinned and murmured, "Yee-ha." She'd made the first hurdle!

SITTING ON THE FENCE, Bart watched Josie bring one of the bays into the corral where she brushed him down, tacked him up and mounted him. Hardly waiting until they'd made one full circle, she put Mack through his paces.

Jog. Walk. Stop. Circle. Tight figure eight. Stop. Back up.

Start over.

She'd chosen well. The horse remained calm and responsive to her every nuance. Bart could hardly see her signals. Moon-Eye was watching from the opposite side of the corral and seemed equally impressed.

"He'll do," Josie said at last. "I'm going to take him for a ride to work out the kinks."

"I'll get the gate." Bart jumped down and opened it for her.

"Any suggestions about where to take him?"

"Follow the rim. Then you can't get lost."

"Oh, he won't lose me."

"It's a big canyon," Bart warned her. "You could ride all day long without ever seeing this place again."

"Well, then, if I'm not back in a half hour, send out the cavalry."

He watched her go, admiring her seat…or maybe it was her pretty little derriere, he decided with a chuckle. He hadn't considered her all that attractive to start, but she certainly was growing on him.

Just then, the sound of an engine caught his attention. He turned as one of the ranch pickups crested a hill and headed straight for them.

"Hey, there's Frank and your kids," Moon-Eye said, moving around the corral to join him.

The truck pulled over and stopped, and a cowboy who was fast approaching middle age got out from behind the wheel. Frank Ewing was short and wiry, and his thin face was nearly overwhelmed by the size of his mustache.

Bart's kids tumbled from the back of the truck where they'd been standing. They had seemed pretty happy until they'd spotted him. Then, as if they'd remembered they were angry with him, they'd both sobered. Now Lainey flounced toward the house without so much as a by-your-leave. Daniel stayed, though he kept some distance behind Frank, who was looking none too happy himself.

"How did it go?" Bart asked.

"We got another problem, boss. The windmill in the far northwest pasture is busted."

"How?"

"Something must've come loose in the head—looks tore up." Frank shook his head. "It was fine last time I was out that way a couple of days ago. Now there's no water for the cows."

"We'd better truck in some, then. Moon-Eye, you fill the tank, and Frank, you see to the tools and any spare parts. Maybe we can patch it up." Figuring this might take a few hours, he said, "Daniel, you'd better get back to the house and let Felice know I'll be late for supper tonight. Tell her to go ahead and serve whether or not I'm back."

It wasn't until his son said, "Sure, Dad," wearing a sour expression, that Bart realized Daniel might have expected to go along with the other men of the ranch.

And it wasn't until they were on their way to the far northwest pasture with the water truck and a box of tools and spare parts that Bart realized a half hour was long gone and so was Josie.

DIRT CHURNING up a yard in front of them made Josie start. The gelding whinnied and backed up, but she quickly got him under control even as she looked around uncertainly.

The earth was blasted along the wash's incline near the horse's head. His protest squealing around the canyon, the bay threw himself upward and tried to unseat her.

Josie fought him, brought him down on all fours. Hands shaking, breath coming too quick, she felt sweat break out all over her body.

"What the heck?" she muttered.

What was going on?

Practically before she could reorient herself, something whined past her and into a boulder perched at the lip of the wash.

The explosion of rock was accompanied by the big bay screaming as he jumped away from the unseen threat.

Josie was frantic...twisting in the saddle...trying to figure out what was happening...missing completely any indication of trouble.

Then she was fighting the bay, trying to get him back under control. The animal was half-crazed, bucking and twisting.

Little left in her, Josie could only hang on.

Chapter Six

Fear ripped through Josie as the bay screamed and jerked and she heard a crack, all seemingly at once.

"Oh, my God!"

Knowing she'd lost all control—that the horse was going down and she with him no matter what she tried—she bailed, body flying....

World turning upside down...dangling from a web of seat belts that stole the breath from her...

She hit solid ground and rolled just before the gelding landed, legs bouncing, head jerking, mane flying into her face. Mere seconds before his body could pin her beneath his awesome weight. Could crush her. Maybe kill her.

The dusty earth of the wash clouded around her. Threatened to smother her. Gag her.

This wasn't happening! Another nightmare.

"Wake up!" she choked out.

But she was already awake and the reality was far worse than any bad dream. The bay was squealing and twisting, fighting back to his feet. What the hell was happening? she wondered frantically.

"Easy, boy, easy." She got to her knees, her movements purposely slow so as not to threaten him. "Calm down, Mack," she said in a singsong, her voice at once purposely sweet and uncontrollably shaky. She darted her gaze to every inch of him that she could see. "You'll be all right."

Was that blood on his hide? From what?

The crack echoed in her head even as Mack found his legs and veered away from her.

A shot...that's what she'd heard...maybe more than just one!

Had Mack taken a bullet? He seemed to be running all right, so maybe a rock had cut him when he'd fallen.

Even so, Josie whipped around, looking for any sign of threat, but as far as she could tell, she was alone. Seemed alone. Sensed she really wasn't. That someone could really be out there with a gun.

Gunning for her?

Still on her knees, Josie felt gripped by fear, and her mind suddenly whirled with terrible visions.

Flashing red-and-blue lights. A beam in her eyes. Couldn't really see them. Eyes closed, mind shutting down. They floated out there, though, just out of reach.

"*Stay with us...be okay...*" Words, all disconnected, floated through her head. "*Get you out...hospital...*"

She tried to answer...screamed at them inside her mind...but they couldn't hear.

Through the ordeal of being lifted, carried, strapped to a board, the pain kept her from leaving completely...reminded her that she had to fight...that she was still alive...

Alive.

But for how long?

Sudden terror drove her as she realized she was in the open, a perfect target.

Tears blurring her vision, Josie crawled along the wash, huddling against the incline, praying that it would be protection from another bullet meant for her. But who? Who hated her enough to want to kill her?

Her memory was returning slowly. Bits and pieces. If only she could force it...

She crawled until her knees stung and her palms felt raw through her thin leather gloves, and the visions inside her head made her want to roll up into a ball and let her mind float away to some safe place....

HE FOUND THE HORSE FIRST—Mack was heading for home, riderless.

Jumping out of the truck, Bart tried to intercept him, but the lathered-up bay danced out of his reach and lengthened his stride, leaving a cloud of reddish dust behind him.

"What the hell..."

So she'd been dumped. Why did that surprise him? Everyone who sat on a horse got dumped occasionally. Only, after seeing Josie on Mack, he was having a hard time imagining it.

Maybe something weird had happened. An accident?

Bart flew into the driver's seat and took off, a curl of fear snaking through his gut.

Thank God instinct had made him turn the water truck around and head back to the house. When he hadn't seen Josie or Mack, he'd sent Frank and

Moon-Eye back out to water the cows and make the repair without him.

Instinct. A man's best friend out here in God's country. He relied on it now to guide him.

Mack had been running parallel to the canyon wall, so undoubtedly Josie had done as he'd suggested and followed the line of the rim. But how far had she gone? From the looks of him, the gelding had worked up quite a head of steam, so Bart went a ways before starting to look for Josie.

The earth here shifted and swung, as did the flow of water during monsoon season. Heavy rains cut swaths through the canyon. The wash dipped and curved, widened and narrowed, all according to the amount of dirt and rock moved by the rushing waters.

Josie could be anywhere. Hurt. Possibly unconscious. He could easily miss her.

Unfortunately the horn on this particular truck was long gone, so he yelled out the open window. "Josie!"

He called her name again…and again…and until his throat felt raw.

No answer.

Likely he couldn't hear her over the truck's engine even if she were calling out to him. He stopped the vehicle and stepped out and away from it.

"Josie, where are you?"

He listened hard. Nothing.

Then he whistled—instinct again—using the same sharp code that she had used to round up the horses. A moment later, the code was returned, the sound clear, if faint. Relief flooded through him. He hadn't even realized how tense he was not knowing what had happened to the woman.

Another exchange and Bart got an idea of Josie's whereabouts, some distance toward the heart of the canyon.

The truck took him closer, but the incline into the wash was far too steep, the earth too loose. He wasn't foolish enough to chance taking the vehicle any farther. Whistling yet again, he descended on foot to an area that was two or three times as deep as he was tall.

When Josie returned the signal, he pinpointed her whereabouts more accurately.

"I've got you!" he yelled, jogging now.

Following a bend in the wash, he saw her coming straight at him. She appeared unhurt if shaky. He had never been so glad to see anyone in his life. He felt as if he'd been holding his breath and just now was able to get much-needed air.

Slowing, he said, "The cavalry has arrived."

"I thought I told you a half hour," she said, attempting the indignant.

At which she failed miserably. She forced a smile, the action defining smudged tracks of dirt on her face, indication that she'd been crying. Her nerves showed raw to Bart.

A very basic instinct bade he take her in his arms to comfort her.

This instinct he fought.

Arms crossed over his chest, he stopped directly in front of her. "Mack passed me like the devil was after him. What happened?"

"I'm not sure." She looked down at her gloved

palms, then wiped them on her filthy jeans. "An accident."

"Tell me."

"Something scared Mack bad" was all she said.

Rather than meet his directly, Josie darted her gaze to some point beyond his left shoulder, as if she was looking for something.

"What?" he pressed, glancing over his shoulder as well, not seeing anything to worry him. "An animal?"

She shrugged. "What does it matter, anyhow? I proved to be as incompetent as you expected, so you can wash your hands of me. I would appreciate a ride back to town, though. I don't think I'd make it on foot right now."

Taken aback, Bart stared at her. "You're giving up?"

"You're not ready to?"

"You think I'd send you packing over a spill?"

"I figured you'd look for an excuse," she admitted, her expression cautiously hopeful at best. "Besides, I wasted your afternoon."

"Let me be the judge of that."

"So this isn't a deal-breaker?"

"We don't have a deal." This time he was the one to add "Yet." Putting an arm around her back, he said, "C'mon, let's get out of here."

He felt her stiffen slightly, but she didn't shrug off his arm. Despite the bravura, she seemed deeply shaken.

Instinct at work again, Bart sensed there was more to Josie's story than she was sharing. Her expertise with horses indicated a long history with them. And anyone with a long history was bound to eat the dust a time or two. No reason to be unnerved, but she was, just as when he'd followed her into the abandoned building.

She'd had an "accident" then, too, he remembered.

Something was definitely wrong, Bart thought, but he wouldn't get anywhere pressing her. Not right now.

He meant to get back to it, though, as soon as he saw an opening.

Reaching the incline, Josie shot ahead a little. But halfway up to the truck, she stepped wrong. Her foot hit loose gravel and she started to slide. She threw a hand out against the fall, but Bart snaked an arm around her waist before she could make contact.

"Gotcha."

"Thanks," she gasped, shuddering as if in pain where he gripped her. "I'm okay."

He loosened the fingers pressed into her ribs. "That you are."

More than okay. She felt great pressed against his side. Again he experienced the overwhelming instinct to pull her into his arms.

And then what?

Unable to help himself, he reached out and brushed a thumb down her cheek to remove the dust. He imagined pulling her closer, cradling her head in his hand and tilting it back so he could study her face up-close-and-personal. He wanted to rub the furrow from her forehead, lick the dried salt from her skin, taste the mysteries of her mouth....

Josie's gray eyes widened, exactly as if she could read his thoughts. Her breathing changed subtly, growing a bit quicker, a bit more shallow.

And a whole lot more exciting than he could stand.

Bart couldn't help himself. He turned imagination into reality. He pulled Josie against him as if she belonged there. She was a little on the thin side for his taste—he generally liked the softness of a fuller woman's flesh—but he knew her fragility was an illusion. A woman unafraid of hard work, she was strong, both in body and in spirit.

Above all, he liked his women spirited.

A wildness deep in her eyes called to him and he answered, skipping the forehead and the cheeks and going directly for her mouth.

At the first touch of his lips to hers, his blood sang. Her mouth was soft if the rest of her wasn't. It opened under his like the petals of some exotic desert flower. He drank at her, tasting her sweet nectar until his head went light and his groin grew heavy.

She fisted his shirtfront, pressed herself closer, kissed him deeper…then, as if catching herself, she gasped and pushed at him.

Bart let go immediately, if with great regret.

Without a word, Josie turned and challenged the incline again, making it to the top in record time. She seemed to have recovered nicely from that case of nerves.

Too bad Bart couldn't say the same. Every nerve in his body was alive.

But what in tarnation did he think he was doing here? He had a ranch to run and two motherless kids to consider. Besides, getting personally involved with someone who worked for him would be damn awkward, so it was out of the question. Or so he tried telling himself.

Suspecting that his life would never be the same for meeting Josie Wales, Bart followed in thoughtful silence.

ON THE WAY BACK TO THE BARN, Bart didn't try to start a conversation, but Josie figured that to be all well and good. She certainly didn't want to talk about that kiss. Not that she expected he would.

He'd just been feeling sorry for her. Poor, pitiful woman who couldn't stay on her horse. Couldn't even stay on her feet. The kiss had been his way of comforting her.

And it had been a mistake, Josie knew, no matter how it had kick-started her pulse, no matter how she'd longed to lose herself in Bart's arms.

The craziness had been momentary. Easy to forget, she assured herself, even as she crossed her arms over her chest to hide a perfectly normal human response to something that never should have happened in the first place.

No, she didn't think Bart would want to talk about that.

What she did fear was that he'd backtrack to the accident. Demand details that she wasn't willing to share.

Gunshots. Had they really happened?

The more she thought about it, the more convinced she was.

If she told Bart, he would either think she was lying to save face, or he would believe her and set a real investigation in motion. He was a lawman at heart if not in fact, after all. She had to keep that in mind.

Not let him get too close.

Not let him get to her.

Racing hormones tended to be distracting and were the last thing she needed in her life right now, Josie decided. She had to keep her head. She had to keep Bart focused on the ranch's future, not on her own past.

That would be the path to disaster, Josie thought. Surely she could keep him from it.

Buildings coming into view offered comfort to a woman who didn't want to be alone with a man. Buildings meant people and she saw a few near the barn. Bart's kids were talking to someone she hadn't yet met.

"Ah, he's here," Bart said. "Over there with Daniel and Lainey. That real cowboy I hired."

As if drawn by the sound of the approaching truck, the cowboy turned to look. He was young and handsome and wore a big smile as easily as he wore his white hat.

Bart stopped the truck and they both got out. Josie was stiff and hurting everywhere. Her bruises now had bruises, she was certain. All eyes in the yard were on them. She bit back the pain she was feeling and tried to act naturally. Bart made the introductions, first the kids, then adult to adult.

"Josie Wales...Will Spencer. You two are gonna be working together."

"Josie, is it?" he asked, a touch of incredulity in his tone.

He appeared about to challenge her, then changed his mind. Will offered his gloved hand for a shake.

When she took it, he gave her an intense stare, his light golden brown eyes narrowing to slits, making Josie wonder if they'd met before.

"Mighty pretty name" was all he said.

And he was a mighty pretty cowboy, she thought, admiring his long, well-muscled lines. Brad Pitt with long curly blond hair and a deep tan. Then it hit her—he was the same cowboy she'd seen sleeping in town just before going into that building after the cat.

"Hey, what happened to Mack?" Daniel demanded.

"We had a little accident," Josie told him.

She could see the gelding in the corral, his saddle removed. He seemed to be all right.

"He was *bleeding,* Dad," Lainey said.

"Actually, the bleeding had already stopped by the time we got him corralled," Will said. "I cleaned him up and medicated the wound. Doesn't look serious, but you'd probably better keep an eye out for infection."

"I need to check on him right now," Josie said.

She wanted a closer look at that wound for a different reason, though at least Will hadn't said anything about a bullet hole. Maybe she'd been wrong and had let her imagination get the best of her.

As she entered the corral, she crooned, "Hey, big boy, how are you doing?"

Mack eyed her but didn't seem particularly concerned with her presence. About to close the gate, Josie realized Bart was directly behind her. The sensation that had overpowered her earlier, that had allowed her to act so crazy, threatened her again.

Sexual tension—she wondered if a person could develop an off switch.

Nerves taut, she crossed to the gelding, who snorted as she drew close. "Mack, I'm not going to hurt you," she murmured. "I just want to take a look."

And though he said nothing, she knew Bart was still standing behind her. She sensed him, almost as if his body were pressing against hers. Her own body responded, momentarily distracting her from her purpose.

Gritting her teeth, she searched desperately for that illusive off switch....

She didn't take her eyes from the horse, nor he off her. For a moment, she feared Mack wouldn't let her get close—he shuffled his feet as if he were thinking about running again—but her continued soft voice and careful movements reassured him. Finally, he settled.

She could see the wound now—a flesh-tearing gash about two inches long and half an inch wide along his shoulder. It appeared raw but clean.

"Odd," Bart said softly, so close that she swore she could feel his breath feather the fine hairs along the side of her face when he spoke. "What could have caused that?"

"A sharp rock—what else?"

"Right, what else?" he echoed, though he didn't sound convinced.

While Bart had no reason to think the wound could have been caused by anything other than a rock, Josie figured a bullet might have grazed him as she'd feared. *Might* being the operative word. Not that she was about to voice that opinion. Then she'd have explaining to do. Rather explaining she *couldn't* do.

"Are you ready to head back to Alcina's?" Bart asked, surprising her.

"You're calling it a day?"

"I'm asking *you.*"

Which meant he was testing her mettle.

Josie wouldn't mind some down time, but she wasn't about to admit as much. She didn't want Bart thinking he'd made a mistake in trying her out…at least not any more of a mistake than she must look to be already.

"I've got a lot of work to do with those horses," she said. "I probably could get to a couple more before dark."

"You're sure you're up to it?"

She had to be. No choice.

"Am I tired?" she said. "Yes, of course. Hurting? You bet." She wasn't about to tell him how much. She would make it through this somehow. "Am I ready to throw in the towel? Not on your life. I *need* this job, Bart, and I'm tougher than I look. Okay?"

Bart seemed downright impressed by her speech. "All right, then." He also looked as if he was pulling back a grin. "But can I make a suggestion?"

"You're the boss."

"Stick close to the barn, would you?"

So he wouldn't have to come after her again?

Josie sighed and muttered, "Exactly what I was planning on doing."

She might be stubborn, but she was no fool.

To Josie's relief, Bart left her to her own devices while he showed his new cowboy around.

Part of her wanted to tell Bart the whole truth. The problem was she didn't know anything for certain herself. She really *didn't* know that she'd been a specific target, even if someone had been shooting at her. Could have been some crazy kid playing around with a gun that he had no business handling. Even as she thought it, she admitted that was a stretch. But if she *had* been a genuine target, she didn't know why.

Add that to the list of things she *didn't* know.

As Josie set about tacking up another horse and testing him out in the corral, she went over in her head what she *did* know for sure.

She had a ranch background, no getting around that. The truck she'd wrecked had been stolen—that she'd been able to gather. While she'd been half-unconscious for some undetermined amount of time, the authorities had been running a check on her fingerprints because of the vehicle. And, after escaping from the hospital, she'd hitched a ride north to Silver Springs with a stranger who'd hardly even spoken to her.

Could someone have followed her? *Who?* Some partner in crime?

Josie's imagination took flight and she tried picturing herself as the female half of a western Bonnie and Clyde team. Maybe she and her lover had robbed a bank and she double-crossed the guy, so now he had it in for her because she'd kept all the money for herself.

Broke as she was, she couldn't even continue thinking of *that* scenario without snorting.

"What's so funny?"

Josie started. She'd been so wrapped up in her

crazy thoughts that she hadn't even realized that Lainey was hanging around to watch her work with the horses.

"Just thinking about me finding myself on foot my first day as Curly-Q's wrangler."

Not exactly a lie.

"I never met a woman wrangler before," Lainey said from her perch at the top of the pipe fence.

"Women can do most jobs men can do," Josie assured her, "no matter what they try to tell you. We females might be lacking in the strength department, but God gave us extra smarts to make up for it. Not that I'd take bragging rights about that around the men."

Grinning, Lainey announced, "I am smarter than my dorky brother. And he's sixteen."

Taking the horse in a figure eight near the fence, Josie noticed the expensive-looking camera that hung from a strap around the girl's neck.

"Fancy piece of equipment you have there."

"Photography's my hobby," Lainey said, touching it lovingly. "This camera belonged to my mom. After she died, Dad said she'd want me to have it."

"I'm sure she would," Josie agreed, knowing the girl would rather have her mother instead.

She must have her mother's looks, Josie figured, seeing no sign of Bart in that red hair, freckled nose or green eyes. Bart's late wife must have been stunning.

"Mom taught me how to use this camera. You know—load the film, take the light reading and everything. It's real old, none of that automatic stuff," Lainey said airily. "But it works great. Mom and I used to go on photo shoots, then later, after the film was developed, we'd pick out the best shots and put them in albums together.''

A lump caught at the back of Josie's throat as she recognized the loneliness and loss in the girl's voice. Somehow she knew it was a loss they shared.

''That's really nice, Lainey. You'll have some wonderful memories every time you open one of those albums.''

Josie would settle for memories. *Any* memories.

The girl's green eyes suddenly filled with tears. Lowering them—undoubtedly so Josie couldn't see—she muttered, ''I think I hear Felice calling me. She probably wants me to help with supper. I'd better go.''

Though Josie hadn't heard anyone call, she let Lainey have her lie. ''I'll probably see you around tomorrow.''

''Yeah, maybe after school.''

The girl's melancholy getting to her, Josie threw herself totally into her work, taking the horse into the pasture and stretching him out, then starting fresh in the corral with a mare.

And all the while, she ignored the pain, telling herself that if she didn't work it out, by morning she would be so stiff that she wouldn't be able to move.

She was just about done for the day when Bart and Will Spencer appeared and watched from the fence. A few minutes later, the pickup carrying Moon-Eye and the cowboy she guessed to be Frank zoomed into view. Bart went off to talk to his men, leaving Will behind.

Josie dismounted and brought the mare back into the corral, where she loosened the cinch on the saddle. Removing the tack and setting it aside, she was aware of Will watching her progress.

"So you call yourself Josie now," he suddenly said, as if he knew she'd once called herself by another name.

Josie pretended indifference, but her insides twisted into a knot. Did Will know her, then? Dear Lord, was she about to learn her true identity?

"What else should I call myself?" she asked breathlessly.

"One name is as good as any, I guess."

He wasn't going to tell her, then? She wanted to scream at him, demand answers.

He asked, "But why the treatment?"

"What treatment?"

"You pretending you don't know me."

Facing him then, she could hardly breathe. He *did* know her. But she made it into a game, hoping he would be the one to slip up.

"*Should* I know you?" she asked, playing with the words.

"It wasn't all that long ago, and you weren't all that drunk," he said, his eyes narrowing again. "You called me Billy Boy, remember? Still could," he added, altering the timbre of his voice so that the flesh on her arms crawled.

Not knowing what else to do, Josie bluffed. "I think you've mistaken me for someone else."

The cowboy stared at her then, as if he was reading her. Josie didn't dare move. Didn't dare breathe. Not until he made his move.

"If that's your story," he finally said, "then I'll go along with it." He started to turn away, stopped, then glanced back over his shoulder. "For now."

Josie's mouth went dry and her heart skipped a beat as he moved off—that was a threat if she ever heard one.

He'd go along with her story *why?*

And for how long?

And what would make him talk?

Chapter Seven

Josie's hands shook as she removed the halter and set the mare back in the larger pasture. Will Spencer's claiming to know her but avoiding the details set her so far on edge that she felt ready to tumble over a cliff.

"Looks like you've had it."

She whipped around to face Bart, who'd sneaked up on her. "And then some."

Her pulse thrummed as he stared at her. His deep blue eyes were the most beautiful thing about his face. And the most dangerous. She felt as if he could look inside of her. Peel her open and read all her secrets. Maybe even the ones she couldn't remember.

"I'll take you into town as soon as you're done here," Bart said, breaking the thread that had been holding her mesmerized. "It's past quitting time."

"I'll just be a few minutes."

As he walked off, Josie wondered if she wasn't giving Bart's obvious interest in her the wrong kind of edge. He had kissed her, after all. Maybe his mind was on something other than work. On something more personal.

Or maybe her mind was, a little voice in her head suggested. She'd already decided that he'd just been feeling sorry for her, and that the kiss had been a mistake. Still, that couldn't make her forget Bart's lips on hers. It couldn't make her deny that, for one short moment, they had connected in a way that thrilled her.

Realizing she wasn't getting done any faster mooning over the situation, Josie concentrated on getting the tack put away and assessing what she needed to do the next day.

Ready in mere minutes as she'd promised, she couldn't help but look for any sign of the new cowboy as she went in search of Bart, who was already waiting for her in the SUV. The barnyard was empty of other people, however. No doubt everyone else was eating supper, including Will, while she herself had no appetite.

Instead, Josie was eating the tension that Will "Billy Boy" Spencer had created, letting it get to her. Her stomach acids were churning and burning her insides. Head against the rest, eyes closed, she tried a little deep breathing to calm herself as they climbed out of the canyon. She couldn't help but wonder if she'd always absorbed life's ills internally.

Not that wondering about anything did her a bit of good. The memories would come when they chose to—nothing she could do to force them.

"You awake?" Bart suddenly asked, startling her to attention.

"Yeah, sure."

She looked around. Out of the canyon and on the

flats already, they were traversing the dirt washboard road toward town.

"I've never heard you so quiet," Bart said, chuckling at his own joke.

"I guess the day plumb wore me out."

He sobered. "I believe the seriousness of your intentions to do a good job, Josie, but you don't have to push yourself further than you can go."

"I'll survive."

"Let's hope so. The Curly-Q hasn't been the death of anyone yet."

Death.

She could have been dead twice in the last week, Josie thought. First the truck, now the horse. Maybe she ought to stick to walking. She was becoming downright accident prone—or always had been and couldn't remember.

She couldn't remember, but what did Will Spencer know about her?

If nothing else, he knew who she was, Josie thought. Knew Josie Wales wasn't her real name. Why hadn't he been more forthright with her? Why play games?

Unless she had somehow given him reason...

For a moment, Josie wondered if her past association with Will had been negative. And if so, whether or not Will had anything to do with those gunshots. He'd had opportunity, that was for certain. He'd shown up at the ranch so conveniently, just as Bart had been driving her back to the barn.

But Will's merely knowing her didn't go hand in hand with his trying to hurt her, she reasoned, especially not when he had acted so friendly.

So what was she to believe?

Jarring her out of her thoughts, Bart said, "I figured maybe you could match Will with a couple of mounts tomorrow," almost as if he knew she was thinking about the cowboy. "I want to get him working with Frank on cutting some of those calves out of the herd as soon as possible."

Her stomach kicked up again at the thought of another confrontation with Will.

"Anything you say, boss."

Whether she was hungry or not, she was going to have to eat or stress would burn a hole right through her.

A thought suddenly struck her—what if Bart knew whatever Will knew about her? Who was to say the cowboy hadn't shared their past with his boss? How likely was that, though? She'd just had that little dance with Will, and he'd as much as promised to go along with her. Surely he hadn't already said anything.

"I figure it'll take you a few days to check out all the horses in the remuda," Bart went on.

"Uh-huh."

"Then you can help with the herd. I planned on doing that myself, but first I need to see about getting that windmill fixed."

"Windmill?"

"The one that normally pumps the well in the northwest pasture. Hauling water all that way is real time-consuming, but we don't have much choice at the moment, so Moon-Eye will take care of that."

She remembered the confab Bart had with his men after they'd returned in the pickup. "So the windmill is what you were talking to your men about a little while ago?"

"Right. Frank and Moon-Eye checked out the situation while you were, uh…otherwise occupied."

Not wanting her accident to become the subject of their conversation, Josie said, "What happened?"

"One of the cotter keys worked its way loose and landed in the gearbox. Frank couldn't figure out how the heck it happened. Anyhow, I guess we had some real wind a few days back—that was when I was still in Albuquerque, packing up my kids. Without that cotter key in place, the fan turned so fast that it did a lot of damage, ripped everything apart— head, pitman arms, gears, helmet."

"Sounds expensive."

"A major expense. A couple of thousand we really can't afford right now, but we need that well."

When it rained, it poured, Josie guessed. Things going wrong all over the place.

The ensuing silence wasn't particularly comfortable, and Josie caught Bart sneaking an intense look at her. She flushed through and through and focused her attention out the side window to cover. Not that she was fooling anyone, leastwise herself. That sexual tension was taking hold of her again, despite her new aches and pains and bruises. Before long, she began wondering what she was getting herself into. And what she might be letting everyone else in for, as well.

She was getting the distinct feeling that she was bad luck and spreading it around. Maybe detouring in Silver Springs had been a mistake. Things were getting too complicated.

They were in sight of Silver Springs when Bart said, "About tomorrow. I'll pick you up at eight or so. I have to run my kids over to the county road where the school bus will pick them up, anyway, so it's only another few minutes into town. That'll work for now.''

''Except that you don't get to eat supper with your family if you drive me home,'' Josie muttered.

''Felice will keep my food hot. And eventually we'll figure out something.''

Eventually. Would she even be around that long?

Josie had thought she'd stay in Silver Springs long enough to save some money. But the way things were getting so complicated, she wasn't sure she'd be there in the morning when Bart came for her.

HEADING FOR HOME, Bart thought about the woman he had held in his arms for too brief a time.

His feelings about her a bundle of contradictions, he nevertheless admitted Josie was the most intriguing woman he'd met since Sara. While his wife had been open and honest, Josie remained elusive, secretive. In some ways, Sara had reminded him of a delicate flower, though once her mind was set on something, she carried through. Beneath her seeming fragility, Josie was *really* tough, both physically and mentally. He wondered if that was by choice or just what she'd learned to do to survive.

She had that air about her, he thought—a startled doe about to run at the first scent of trouble.

She hadn't run when he'd kissed her, though, not at first. And no matter how he tried to shake the memory, it wouldn't leave him be. He'd been at loose ends since Sara had been killed. No other woman had so much as caught his attention since then. Until now.

He had to be crazy. He was starting a new life with new responsibilities. He had a ranch to run and kids to raise. He didn't have time to get involved with a woman—especially one about whom he knew nothing.

That bothered him still—Josie's reluctance to give up any details of her past. If he *were* to get involved, he'd want to know everything there was about her, and he was betting she wasn't willing to give it up.

And then there was Mack. Not that he faulted Josie for having a riding accident.

But that wound…that *did* bother Bart.

If he didn't know better, Bart would say Mack had been grazed by a bullet. But if someone had been shooting at them, Josie would surely have said so.

Unless she'd had her own reasons for leaving out that little detail….

But how to find out the truth.

It all came back to Josie herself, he suspected, and with or without her cooperation, he was going to have to learn more about her. Luckily, with his background in law enforcement, that wouldn't be too difficult. He could easily call in a few favors. She wouldn't have to know a thing about it, either.

Not if she had nothing to hide, that was.

But…what if she did?

That thought instigated a whole new problem.

He'd brought his kids to the Curly-Q to keep them away from trouble and bad influences. He surely wasn't going to invite danger around them.

One thing at a time, Bart told himself. He would see what he could dig up before making any decisions. He'd start with the Motor Vehicle Division first. If Josie so much as had a parking ticket, he would know for what and how much.

Dark had settled around the old adobe by the time he parked. Lights were on in both Daniel's and Lainey's rooms. They were no doubt both getting themselves ready for their first day at their new schools. He'd offered to take them himself, to get them settled in properly. They'd quickly set him straight on that idea. They didn't need to be embarrassed by their dad holding their hands—they weren't babies.

He might have expected that of Daniel, but when had Lainey gotten so grown-up without him realizing it? he wondered.

Entering the house, Bart was surprised to find his father in the living room, ensconced in his favorite chair, television blaring.

"Hey, Pa, shouldn't you be in bed resting?"

The old man waved his hand at Bart and used the remote to click off the set. "I'm tired of resting," he complained. "That's all I've been doing ever since you arrived. I got more important things on my mind. I was waiting for you to get back. I hear we got trouble."

Bart's thoughts immediately shifted back to Josie's problem with Mack. Did his father know something about that wound that he didn't? "Who says?"

"Moon-Eye told me about the windmill."

"Oh, that."

"Oh, that?" his father echoed. Voice rising, he demanded, "What else has gone wrong?"

"Settle down, Pa. Nothing to worry about. First thing in the morning, I'm going to call Rodriguez to bring out his truck and a crew."

"Rodriguez? Are you crazy? Do you know how much he'll charge us?"

"Frank says he's the best—he's seen Rodriguez at work."

"I say use Driscoll."

Bart folded his arms across his chest. "Who did you say was running operations on this ranch?"

Emmett got all red-faced and began sputtering. The sputters turned to a wheezy cough that made Bart's insides tighten. He was about to rethink his challenge when his father said, "You're in charge, son, just like I said."

"Then I'm using Rodriguez."

Bart waited for his father to get in another jab, but somehow the old man kept himself in check. He was on his best behavior.

"I know getting the windmill running again is a big expense, Pa, but it's not going to break us."

"Not that alone, maybe," Emmett muttered darkly. "As long as things don't *keep* going wrong like they've been doing."

"You make it sound like an epidemic," Bart said.

His father appeared about to say something more, then thought better of it. He clenched his jaw, pulling his lips into a tight line exactly the way Lainey did when she didn't want to talk something out.

And Bart started to get a sinking feeling.

What, exactly, was his father *not* telling him?

THE HOUSE WAS FINALLY QUIET.

Having slept a few hours after soaking in a hot tub, dosing herself with ibuprofen and eating the meal that Alcina had so thoughtfully left for her, Josie rose. She felt a whole lot better—not nearly as achy as she'd suspected she would be, and a lot more clear-headed. She knew what she had to do.

"I've got to be leaving now," she told Miss Kitty, who'd been sleeping with her and now watched from the middle of the rumpled bed. "It's best for everyone. I only wish I could take you with me."

She fetched the leather bag from the corner of the room, then gathered her meager possessions from the closet and dresser and set all on the bed. Miss Kitty had to investigate, of course, and Josie had to gently remove the cat from the bag so she could pack.

"I am going to miss you," she murmured.

A pang coursed through her as she thought about leaving the animal behind. Only two days and already she felt as if she were abandoning an old friend. But the cat had an owner somewhere, she reminded herself, setting her underwear and socks in the bottom of the bag. And she'd put up all those signs.

Besides, under the circumstances, she would do well just to take care of herself.

Shirts next—Josie folded them carefully so they wouldn't wrinkle and thought how she just couldn't be responsible for a helpless animal on the road. She didn't have a clue as to how far she would go or where she would end up—only that she had to get out before something terrible happened.

She worked faster, throwing in a small cloth bag of toiletries, a leather bag holding her spurs, a cotton sweater and a pair of jeans. Running her hands over the clothing to smooth any wrinkles, she felt an odd lump. Curious, she tracked the lump to the fifth jeans pocket—the one perfect for holding coins.

Only it wasn't a coin she removed, but a small fancy silver pin, initials inscribed in the middle.

"N-B-R-A?"

Wondering if this could be a clue to her identity, Josie thought hard, but nothing came to her. In the end, she shook her head and returned the pin to the pocket.

With a lump in her throat, she kissed the cat and rubbed those soft ears she loved one last time. "Alcina won't throw you to the coyotes, so don't worry."

She felt guilty about saddling Alcina with the responsibility she had taken on, but if someone got hurt because of her, she'd feel even worse.

That was the crux of the matter, she told herself. People getting hurt. Her. Anyone around her. Maybe even Alcina. She had no choice.

With regret, she left the tiny room—the only home she could even remember. Thinking to take some rolls or crackers in case her stomach fired up, she set the bag and her hat in the mudroom and entered the kitchen. She practically ran into Alcina, who was lifting a steaming kettle from the stove.

"Can't sleep, either?"

"Alcina!" Josie was at a loss—the last thing she wanted was to have to explain herself.

"I thought some tea might help." Alcina filled a pot with hot water. "Join me?"

"Uh, sure."

"Let's take it into the parlor."

Adding an extra cup and saucer to the tray, Alcina led the way and sat on the couch, whose upholstery was barely a shade darker than the blonde's silk wrapper. Even ready for bed, Alcina had an elegance that matched her surroundings.

An itchy Josie perched on the side chair. She wanted to get going. Now here she was trapped for the moment.

Alcina had barely poured the tea when she asked, "So, where are you headed? You *are* in the process of leaving, aren't you?"

Josie gaped at the other woman. "I, um, yeah, I was…am."

Alcina concentrated on her cup for a moment, taking a few sips before murmuring, "Mmm, that's soothing," as if nothing were wrong. "Nothing like a nice cup of tea to put things into perspective."

"Yeah, right," Josie muttered, taking a swallow and feeling not a whit better for it.

Looking up from her cup, Alcina fixed Josie with her gaze. "How much trouble are you in?"

"I'm not in—"

"Don't bother denying it. I've sensed something was wrong since I found you standing on my porch. Maybe talking about it would help."

The lie that Josie wanted to tell just wouldn't surface. "I don't want to involve you," she said. It was the best she could offer.

"Honey, I'm already involved. I *want* to be involved." Alcina laughed. "Is it a man? Did he hurt you? Those bruises came from somewhere."

As did the vision prompted by Alcina's question.

Open hand flashing toward her face…contact driving back her head…

A new surge of fear shot through Josie as she said, "There *was* a man…"

Not that she could see him in her mind's eye, though. She could *feel* him. Knew he existed without being able to remember more.

"Where did you think to run this time?"

"I—I didn't think," Josie admitted.

"Then why leave?"

She took a big breath. "Because he may be here."

That's what she'd been fearing without being able to define it. No doubt that's why she'd been so jumpy all along. Her subconscious was aware of danger following her.

"You've seen him?"

"Maybe. I can't be sure." She needed to tell someone, Josie decided. "I can't remember."

Alcina's brow furrowed. *"Can't?"*

"An accident. The truck I was driving went off the road…not that I exactly remember. Only little bits and pieces. I woke up in the hospital a few days later, I think, without a clue. I don't even know my real name."

"The authorities couldn't help?"

"I—I didn't wait for them to find out. I took off, hitched a ride." She certainly couldn't admit she'd stolen a truck or that the authorities had run her fingerprints through their computers—she'd overheard them talking about it. "Maybe it wasn't the right thing to do, but I was confused and scared."

Again, Alcina stared at her. "Is that because of *him?* The man?"

"I—I guess," Josie hedged, not at all certain that wasn't the truth.

Instinctively, she could have been running from the very person who'd put her in that hospital bed.

That same person who'd shot at her that afternoon.
He could have been trying to cause another accident.
A *fatal* accident. He could have missed on purpose,
hoping the horse would throw her and that she'd
break her neck.

"What makes you think this man, whoever he is,
might be here?"

Josie shook her head and backed off, fearing that,
if she put words to her worry, Alcina would do
something drastic like call in the authorities herself.
By now they had a line on her via those fingerprints—at the very least there was the stolen truck
to account for—and she wasn't ready to face the
consequences, not when she couldn't even remember enough to make her own defense.

Josie sweated out the uncomfortable silence.
What now?

"You'll have to stop running and face your fears
sometime," Alcina finally said.

"You make it sound like my running away from
things is a habit."

"Isn't it?"

"No—"

"You ran from trouble at the hospital, and now
you want to run from it here. How many other
times?"

To her shame, Josie suspected it might be more
times than she cared to admit. Alcina might have
her pegged. That she was a coward, making excuses
as to why she had to leave, when in reality, she was
running from a past that she was only starting to
remember—and only in bits and pieces.

If she stayed put, would the truth all come back

to her? And if it did, could she deal with those memories, whatever they were?

"Besides, you have no money," Alcina continued, sounding incredibly reasonable. "You'll have
to hitch a ride and be at fate's mercy. Don't do that
to yourself, please. At least here you have a place
to stay, a way to make money and good people you
can count on. You won't be alone. That's a whole
lot more than a lot of unlucky souls in this world
can say."

Knowing Alcina was making all the sense in the
world, Josie sighed. Deep down, she didn't really
want to leave. She didn't want to be alone.

"I can try to break bad habits," she said. "All
right, I'll stay put for a while."

"Good. And if you need help, you'll ask for it,
right?"

Being that she wasn't sure about that, Josie was
glad her friend didn't press her. A smiling Alcina
covered a yawn and set her cup on the tray.

Rising, she said, "I think I can get some sleep
now."

"Me, too." At least Josie hoped so or she would
never make it through the day working for Bart. She
took the tray from Alcina. "I'll take care of this on
my way to bed."

Once in the kitchen, she set the tray on the
counter. The last thing she expected when she turned
around was to come face-to-face with Tim Harrigan.

"Jeez!" Her hand shot to her breast where her
heart palpitated. Where in the heck had he come
from? "You nearly scared the life out of me!"

"Sorry. I did say something, but I guess you were
preoccupied and didn't hear."

She noted he was dressed in street clothes—jeans, shirt, mud-caked boots—if not wearing his hat. His light brown hair spilled over his forehead as if wind-blown.

"You just came in?" she asked.

"A while ago." Tim's forehead creased, showing his concern. "Listen, Josie, let me be honest here. I overheard you and Alcina talking."

"What did you hear?" she snapped, appalled.

Alcina she trusted; Tim she wasn't so sure about.

"Whoa!" Frowning, he backed up. "Take it easy."

But she remembered how he'd stopped on the stairway to listen before, and she wondered if he eavesdropped wherever he went. Had he heard the whole conversation, including her confessing to having amnesia, to fearing that some faceless man was after her?

"Josie, if you really want to leave Silver Springs...well, I do have a truck and can take you anywhere you want to go."

"Why would you?"

"I'm at loose ends. No commitments, nowhere to go myself. As for money, I can spare a couple of hundred—if that's what you need to help make up your mind."

Josie's natural suspicions continued to rise, making her say, "You don't even know me and you're willing to lend me money?"

"Give, not lend. Look, you seem to be a nice person who just happens to be down on your luck... I know how crummy that can be. It would make me feel good to give someone who needs it a helping hand."

He seemed so sincere, Josie wondered if she should feel guilty for suspecting him. "What are you?" she asked, trying to make light of the situation. "A do-gooder who drives from town to town, looking for the neediest person?"

"Someone gave me a helping hand once. I'd just like to pass on that kindness. That's all. No strings, I promise. I'm just a guy who has nothing to his name but a decent truck and some bucks in my pocket. No life to speak of." He frowned. "No wife. No home."

"Your wife died?"

"Divorced me. She thought she could change me into something I wasn't, and when that didn't happen…let's just say I was history and she was already on to the next guy."

No wonder he was wandering, Silver Springs being as good as the next place for him to stay awhile. "I'm sorry marriage didn't work out for you, Tim."

"Not as sorry as I am." He sighed. "So, if there's someplace you want to go, you say the word and I would be honored to get you there."

For a moment, Josie was torn. Escape was sounding really good right now. But escape from what?

Physical danger…or complications?

Naturally, Bart's visage came immediately to mind.

"Talking to Alcina really did change my mind. I'm staying for now."

"Well, the offer is open-ended…for as long as *I* stick around, that is."

"I'll remember."

Tim nodded. "Good night, then."

"'Night."

He headed for the front of the house and the stairs.

Josie didn't immediately leave. Still thinking about Tim's tempting offer, she set the dirty cups and saucers in the dishwasher.

If she ran, what would she accomplish? Whoever was after her might just follow. Then what? She had to take a stand sometime. Fight for her memories. Fight for herself.

And in the process, she had to make certain she didn't bring disaster down on the people who were being good to her. That was the real trick. She prayed this was one challenge she could meet head-on.

After washing the fancy teapot by hand and setting it in the drain, Josie headed into the mudroom, picking up her bag and hat on the way to her temporary home.

Entering the ironing room, she flipped on the light, saying, "Well, Miss Kitty, looks like you haven't lost me yet, after all."

Strange. Usually the cat rushed to greet her, but Miss Kitty was nowhere in sight.

"Miss Kitty? Where are you, sweetheart?"

A smothered complaint from beneath the bed revealed the cat's hiding place. Her reaction to a sensed abandonment?

Josie got down on her knees, lifted the cover and ducked her head to see. Sure enough, fur fluffed out, the cat was scrunched against the wall.

"Come over here, you rascal."

When she reached for Miss Kitty, the cat hissed and moved farther away.

Acting just as she had in the abandoned building,

Josie realized, the hair on her arms prickling. She sat back on her heels and looked around the room, but nothing was out of place. She'd left the shade up on the window near the bed. Had someone looked in, scaring the cat?

She was having that feeling again....

And was that movement she saw outside? She swore she saw moonlight glinting off something pale.

Heart pounding, Josie flew to her feet and rushed out of the room, through the mudroom and out the door to the yard. Crazy thoughts raced through her head. Determined to confront her own danger and be done with it, she looked around frantically. Her poor night vision prevented her from seeing much but hulking shadows.

Trying to convince herself that nothing was wrong, that she'd merely spooked herself by discussing her situation with Alcina, then having Tim pop out of the woodwork to give her a start, Josie returned to the house and to her room. And while Miss Kitty didn't seem as relaxed as usual, the cat was standing in the middle of her bed, waiting.

"There you are," Josie murmured, trying to sound natural and running a hand through the fur, setting the cat to purring. "Everything is all right."

Even as she spoke the words, she couldn't stop herself from giving one last, long look out the window.

But if danger lurked in those shadows, it chose to elude her...for now.

Chapter Eight

When Bart picked up Josie the next morning, the first thing he said when she climbed into the truck was, "I see you're moving pretty good."

"Better than I expected."

A hot shower had loosened stiff joints and another ibuprofen dulled the ache.

"Glad to hear it. I wasn't sure if you would be wanting to move at all after yesterday."

"Like I had a choice," she muttered as he headed the SUV for the Curly-Q. "So your kids are off to their new schools. I'll bet they're nervous."

"Them and me. I want this thing to work. I figure if they like their school and make new friends fast, my job will be that much easier."

"It's got to be tough raising kids alone—especially when one of them is a teenager."

"Tough but rewarding."

With Josie prompting him, Bart spent the better part of the ride telling her about the trials and tribulations and joys of single parenthood.

She loved listening to him, and yet the conversation left her feeling at odds. Dissatisfied. Wondering if, through her accident, she could have forgotten kids of her own. Surely a mother could never forget the existence of her own children. Recognizing an empty spot inside herself, she wondered if Bart really knew how lucky he was.

Josie envied Bart his big family, despite the problems that he'd hinted at having with his father and brothers. She'd give anything for the sense of belonging he must have.

She'd give anything to belong to *him*.

Startled by that unexpected turn of thought, Josie fought sudden panic.

It was a longing in general to be part of things that she missed, she assured herself. Maybe she was and just couldn't remember.

But she didn't *feel* part of things, didn't feel any connection except to Bart. She'd felt connected to him all along—just not the ever-after kind of connection. How could it be serious after a couple of days and a single kiss? Probably it would never happen, which was good.

She never wanted any man to have control over her, not ever again, Josie thought, irritated with herself.

What had she been thinking?

By the time Bart brought the SUV to a stop at the side of the house, Josie was mired in a strange mood.

"We have a new hire coming out this morning," he told her. "Name's Peter Dagget. He's young, but he's had some summer experience moving cattle, so I agreed to give him a try."

"That means first thing I have to match two men with the right horses."

"I'm not worried about Will," Bart said. "After

busting broncos on the rodeo circuit, he can probably handle whatever you send his way. Pay special care that Peter gets a ride he can handle, though.''

''Got it, boss.''

Josie meant to pay special care to more than choosing mounts. Instincts bristling, she would keep an eye out for any sign of trouble. She didn't mean to get ambushed again.

Though Will did his best to try it.

Bart had disappeared into the house—said he had to make arrangements about that windmill—and she was putting a palomino named Pretty Girl through her paces, when Will's voice sang through the fence at her.

''You two look good together,'' he said appreciatively, ''but nothing like you do on that sorrel of yours. Whatever happened to her?''

Pulse triggered by the reference to the horse she'd dreamed about and even now could see in her mind's eye, Josie let herself be distracted for a moment.

Flaxen mane whipping in her face, she made a tight turn and took the straightaway....

A moment being long enough for the mare she was riding now to test her. Pretty Girl bolted to one side, then twirled on her hindquarters. And all the while, a grinning Will leaned over the fence where he'd climbed up to watch.

''Oh, no, you don't,'' Josie muttered under her breath.

She sat fast, held the mare together with firm legs and a steady hand, collected her and took her once around the corral. Then she walked the horse to the gate and unhooked it. Pretty Girl tried being stubborn about not wanting to go through the opening, but Josie won that contest. In the end, they pranced right through.

"Ah, you found one with some life in her," Will said.

"And Pretty Girl is all yours for the day."

As she dismounted, the cowboy came down off the fence to take the reins from her.

"I like my horses fast." Will fixed her with his golden gaze and lowered his voice. "Just like my women."

Refusing to acknowledge the personal message he was telegraphing with that suggestive look and tone, Josie said, "Then you can give each other a good workout."

Will tipped his white hat. "Don't mind if I do, ma'am."

Without so much as using a stirrup, he launched himself into the saddle and put the mare through her paces much like Josie herself had, only sharper and faster and a little less careful. Bart's bronco-busting comment came to mind as she watched Will show off—for trying to impress her certainly seemed to be his game.

The rodeo circuit. He was a natural.

Is that where they'd met? Is that where he'd seen her on the sorrel?

The desire to ask became overwhelming.

Myriad questions burned on her tongue, but Josie held them back. If Will meant her harm, she wanted to find a way to make him show his hand. Instinctively, she suspected being too direct with a spoiler would be a serious mistake.

Still, it was killing her—how well *did* they know each other?

Just then, Moon-Eye left his quarters accompanied by Frank, A.C. and D.C. The men and dogs headed straight for her, Frank picking up the reins of an already-saddled horse he'd left out to graze. She recognized the bay as one of their escorts when Bart had brought her onto the ranch.

"She feels good," Will said, bringing the mare to a halt inches from Josie. "She'll do."

"I'm so glad you approve," Josie muttered.

"Well, would you look at that," Moon-Eye called as the men drew closer. "That palomino is *almost* as pretty as the cowboy riding her."

Will grinned and tipped his hat so that sunlight glinted off his golden curls. "A man with a sharp eye."

"You and me better move out, Will," Frank said, swinging himself up into the saddle. Then, to Josie, "That Dagget kid should be here any time. You fix him up with a mount and send him to the far north pasture after us."

He gave her instructions on how the new hire should get there, then led the way out, whistling for the cattle dogs, who tore off ahead of him and quickly disappeared over a rise.

If she had expected Will to have anything more to say to her, Josie would have been disappointed. Without so much as a look her way, he caught up with Frank and rode with him as if they were old buddies.

At least he was keeping his word pretending he didn't know her, she thought.

"If anyone needs me," Moon-Eye said, heading

for the row of ranch trucks near the storage shed, "I'll be hauling out more water to that northwest pasture. Them girls was pretty thirsty yesterday."

Josie waved him off, then went about the task of rounding up a suitable horse for the new hire—a gelding paint she'd checked out the day before. Native was older and a little lazy—he tended to need some encouragement to go. He wouldn't have been her first choice but for Bart's warning.

As she tacked him up, her mind wandered.

Gaze focused sharp through the flaxen mane, she applied leg pressure and the sorrel mare whipped around the first barrel.... "Barrel," Josie murmured, cinching Native's saddle.

She dug in the coin pocket of her jeans and pulled out the pin she'd found the night before. She stared at it, knowing this was a key to her identity.

"NBRA..." It took her only a few seconds. "National Barrel Racing Association."

If this pin belonged to her, she was a barrel racer! That would explain her natural affinity with horses. Excitement pulsed through her. Holding on to the pin, she conjured the vision again, hoping she could take it further this time.

But her concentration was broken by the sound of a reedy engine. Eyes open once more, she spotted a motorbike shoot down the road toward the canyon floor. Peter Dagget, no doubt. He was catapulting over rough areas so fast that he seemed to be flying in places.

She sure didn't want him handling one of her mounts like he did the bike—like some daredevil out of control.

Josie stuck the pin back in her jeans pocket for later.

Leading Native, she stepped out of the corral, continuing to watch as the loose horses followed the motorbike at a safe distance. They were obviously nervous. Native, too, was bothered by the noise approaching so fast. He tried dancing away from her when it seemed the bike was going to keep going. The rider barely slowed in time to stop a foot short of Josie, an accompanying whirl of red dust making her cover her nose and mouth so she wouldn't suck it all in.

Cutting the engine, a tall, skinny kid hopped off, saying, "Hey, where can I find Bart Quarrels?"

Josie blinked against the settling dust and took a good look at his loopy grin. "You must be Peter Dagget. Don't ever ride your bike into the canyon like that again. The horses don't like it. More important—*I* don't like it."

Peter made a weird face. "Uh-oh, you the missus?"

"I'm the wrangler—Josie Wales." She grabbed Native's reins and turned him around. "And this is your mount for the day."

"That scrawny little fella? He doesn't look like he's got any life in him at all." Peter looked around at the loose horses that were coming in closer now. "That one." He pointed to the blue roan. "I want to ride her."

"Juniper? She's just green-broke. No one can ride her yet."

"I bet *I* can."

"Not unless I say so, you can't." She held out

Native's reins. "You'd better catch up to the men and fast."

Peter mounted Native, all the while sending longing looks at Juniper—what Josie thought of as horse-lust. He really was young, just a teenager, little older than Bart's son. She repeated the directions Frank had given her. The young cowboy nodded and goosed Native to get going. He didn't even try to hide his frustration at the horse's naturally slow pace.

Then, when he gave him a stronger kick and called the horse a few choice names, she yelled after him, "That horse better not come back with bruised sides! And you treat him with the respect he deserves!"

"Yes, ma'am!" Peter returned, his shoulders folding slightly, as if he were well and truly chastised.

Josie figured him to be a kid with more enthusiasm than experience, a big mouth but not really a mean sort. She watched until he disappeared from view.

Then, sensing a presence behind her, she whipped around, pulse thrumming...but it was only Juniper, come to bother her for a little attention.

"So, should I have let young Peter ride you?" she asked, reaching out to stroke the mare's neck.

Juniper blew hard through her nose.

"I'll take that as a 'no, thanks,'" Josie murmured, working at removing a tangle from the mare's mane. "Besides, I intend to ride you before I let anyone else do it." Realizing that statement had the sound of permanence about it, she sighed and gave the roan's neck a pat. "But not today, sweetheart, not today. I have other horses to check out first.''

As she approached the pasture adjacent to the barn, she gave a series of sharp whistles. Several horses responded with whinnies. Even so, she felt a bit adrift. Because the yard was barren of people, and if she didn't know better, the house might be, as well?

Or simply because Bart was nowhere in sight?

She felt alone.

A little spooked, aware of exactly how alone she was in her secrets, Josie figured she'd better grow eyes in the back of her head if she wanted to stay safe.

ONLY HALFWAY THROUGH the morning and already Bart had a headache. To start, he'd taken his first look at the books. No wonder the Curly-Q was in trouble.

He'd already known some of it. Based on the high beef prices of the seventies, his father had borrowed money at double-digit rates on the inflated price of the land, bringing the cost of the ranch far beyond its realistic value. He'd purchased new equipment and had expanded the herd. Then the drop in beef prices and land values of the eighties had meant near disaster. Scores of ranches throughout the West had gone broke and out of operation, most selling to corporations or ranchers who hadn't taken such a risk.

Somehow his father had been able to avoid total disaster. It had been touch-and-go for years, but Emmett Quarrels had hung on—by his fingernails, as Bart saw it. While he'd been able to manage to stay afloat alone, he hadn't asked his sons for a thing. But now something else was happening—a string of expensive bad luck over the past six months and a serious health problem that had backed the old man into a corner.

No wonder Pa had made that comment about things going wrong, Bart thought.

He knew the ranch couldn't survive going on as it had been during the past years. They were two years behind in mortgage payments now. Serious changes would have to be made...but one thing at a time.

His immediate problem was getting enough help. Maybe he ought to hire some extra day workers until Reed and Chance decided whether they were in or out of the deal. That, of course, would take more money, and until they sold off some of the herd they were pretty much cash-strapped.

Therein lay the catch-22.

Which was why he started off in a mood to beat all get-out.

Then, after talking to his contact at the Motor Vehicle Division twice, Bart found himself with an even bigger headache than before. It seemed that Miss Josie Wales did not have a driver's license, not in New Mexico. Neither was there a record of any Josephine or Jocelyn or Joelle Wales. His friend had checked for *any* woman with that particular last name. He'd come up with a new driver—a teenager—several who were middle-aged and one who was nearly eighty.

After which, his friend had gotten *his* contacts to run computer checks in neighboring states. Also to no avail. Bart had found no one who could be his Josie.

His Josie?

Bart didn't know why, but that's the way he was starting to feel—as if he had some claim. Otherwise, why would he be so worried about something bad happening to her? Why was he going to all this trouble to dig up information that she wasn't willing to give him herself?

He tried telling himself it was just the lawman in him—Pa had said he wouldn't be able to shake that part of himself and so might as well put it to use. And so he had.

His Josie...

With so many worries on his mind, Bart didn't need this one to compound things. He needed to get into Taos to pick up some supplies that were unavailable in Silver Springs.

And he couldn't forget to take in Lainey's film to be processed—his daughter had already shot a new roll in addition to the one that had been in her camera when they'd arrived. He'd take them to one of those quick processing places and surprise her with the prints when she got home from school. That ought to put a smile on her freckled face, he thought, as his own lips quirked.

He needed something to feel positive about, that was for certain.

On the way to his vehicle a quarter of an hour later, Bart saw Josie was working an Appaloosa just outside the corral.

No matter his determination, he couldn't resist.

As if drawn by a magnet, Bart found himself wandering over to her. That she was a superior horsewoman was evident. He'd seen firsthand her soft heart in the way she'd rescued and treated Miss Kitty. Neither of those qualities would hold up in his book if he couldn't trust her, though.

Wondering if he could, desperately wanting to, Bart was caught by Josie's instant smile when she spotted him. Her pleased expression flooded him with a warmth that was contrary to his purpose.

"Did you get what you needed?" she asked, turning the Appaloosa as he came alongside her.

For a moment, he thought about how he needed *her*. Then he started as a suspicion occurred to him—could she possibly know that he'd been investigating her identity?

"Depends on what we're talking about," he ground out.

"The repair to the windmill."

"Oh, that. Yeah, I'm set there."

Josie dismounted and tossed the horse's reins over a rail. When she stepped closer, her very proximity distracted him. Gazing deeply into her soft gray eyes, he had a difficult time wanting to play games with her. But she'd left him with no choice.

"I was rethinking your transportation situation," he began.

Her smile dimmed. "Too complicated, huh?" Her expression despondent, she glanced away. "Well, working for you was nice while it lasted. I guess that leaves me with some decisions to make."

Wondering what those decisions might be, Bart said, "You don't understand. I figured another way to get you here. We've got a junker of a truck we don't use for anything. Pa bought it a few months back for spare parts but hasn't had time to strip it yet. The body's rusting out, the tires are nearly bald, the starter's a little tricky, but it still goes. While the weather holds, at least, it'd get you back and forth between Alcina's and the ranch.''

Bart found himself responding to Josie's renewed smile in ways he didn't want to consider too closely. He couldn't let her get to him now or he'd never pull this off.

''Sounds good,'' she said.

Steeling himself for what he had to do, Bart somehow wore his best poker face as he said, ''You have a driver's license, right?''

''Of course I do.''

''Then I'll need to see it…for insurance purposes.''

''Oh.''

Bart waited.

Trust, he thought—he wanted to be able to trust her. His spirits flagged as he watched her eyes closely. They grew shadowed with some internal weight, and he could practically see her wheels spinning.

Still smiling, if looking a bit uncomfortable, she asked, ''You don't have to see my license right now, do you?''

''Before you get behind the wheel of the truck, I do.''

''You already let me drive one of your trucks yesterday when we rounded up the horses.''

''But that was here on Curly-Q property.''

''Right.'' Those wheels were spinning even more rapidly. ''I, uh, don't have my license on me, though. It's back at Alcina's, somewhere in my bag.''

Did that mean she didn't have one—or that she did but under a different name? He wanted to ask her, to be direct. But more, he wanted the truth and he didn't believe she was ready to give it up yet.

So Bart found himself backing down. "Well, you can show it to me later, then." He took one last shot. "It's a New Mexico license, right?"

She hesitated only a second before echoing him. "Right."

Nodding, Bart wondered what excuse she would use later when she couldn't produce a New Mexico license. Or one with the name Josie Wales. She was lying to him. It seemed he couldn't trust her, after all.

"I need to be off," he said coolly, already moving away from her. "I'm running up to Taos for supplies. Anything I can get you?"

Glancing back, he was caught by her expression—for the moment, too open, too vulnerable. Then she shook herself, closed herself off from him.

"I've got everything I need right now," she said. "But thanks."

A disappointed Bart drove off, wondering if her real name would suit her nearly as well as the one she'd borrowed....

EMMETT WATCHED out his bedroom window as Barton's vehicle pulled out of the yard. The only other person he could see was that young woman his oldest had hired to work with the horses.

She sat one pretty good, he decided, though he'd like nothing better than to see her off his place and fast. He wasn't too old to recognize the signals when a man was sniffing around a female—he'd seen Barton's posturing around the wrangler earlier and the day before, as well. That didn't suit Emmett's plans, at all. He wanted Barton to concentrate on Alcina Dale.

That way, when the bank came a-calling for those back mortgage payments and they didn't have the wherewithal to answer properly, he'd have leverage with her daddy. Tucker Dale had once been his partner. Now the old coot was too tied up in his fancy bank to remember the old days, when they'd been friends.

But if Barton and Alcina were an item, Tucker would have to rethink his position. The banker might even be willing to make one of those back mortgage payments himself as a wedding present, Emmett mused. Tucker ought to be that grateful to any man who finally made an honest woman of his daughter—her biological clock running out, and all.

He looked for Barton's vehicle again and got a glimpse of it on the road out of the canyon just before it disappeared over the rim.

"Finally, a man can have free reign on his own place for a while," Emmett muttered and left his bedroom for his office

Then, again, he'd put himself in this situation.

It had all started with that danged letter.

The phone rang, jolting him out of that dark memory, but Felice got it from some other part of the house.

Sitting at his heavy wooden desk in his high-backed leather chair, Emmett opened his fancy cigar box with the ritual of a man who didn't get to do what he wanted when he wanted any more. He pulled out a cigar, which he smelled and lit and puffed with a great deal of pleasure.

But before he could get out to the barn and really enjoy himself taking charge with the hired help— firing her, that was—a knock at the office door stopped him.

"Mr. Emmett? I know you're in there. I can smell the cigar smoke."

"What is it, Felice? No more of your lectures."

"The phone—it's for you."

"Got it." He picked up the receiver. "Quarrels here."

"Mr. Quarrels," came a female voice from the other end. "This is Lena Little Bird from Azure Skies Realty in Taos. I understand that you're in the market to sell your—"

"I'm not in the market now and never will be!" he shouted into the phone. "The Curly-Q is not some trade-in! Why can't you people stop bothering me?"

"I-I'm very sorry—"

He slammed the receiver into its cradle before the woman could finish her apology.

"Damn real estate agents!"

He'd been waiting for this follow-up to the wind-mill's needing major repair. After each incident had come a phone call...an inquiry as to whether the Curly-Q was for sale. The voices at the other end were always different—as were the realty companies involved. But the call always came.

Another knock was immediately followed by the door swinging open. Felice was standing there, arms crossed, staring at his cigar disapprovingly. "Keep that up and..."

"I don't need to hear it!"

Emmett wouldn't take anything from anyone else. But Felice and him—well, they had an understanding. She was the only one he ever let boss him around. Probably because she was the only one who ever stuck it out. Her and Moon-Eye.

"I have something on my mind," she said, no-nonsense as usual. "You brought Mr. Bart back here to run this place—let him run it."

"What else *have* I been doing?"

"Lulling him until he's committed," she said. "You made him a deal, now you stick with it. He's got enough on his mind, what with those kids so unhappy and you dying and all."

They were at an impasse. Always smart enough to know when to back off, however, Emmett nodded. "Good enough."

There went his plans to fire Josie Wales. Barton wouldn't like it and wouldn't be afraid to say so. Then Felice would feel justified getting in on the act.

Damn!

"Well, don't you have work to do?"

Nodding, Felice stepped forward to take the cigar from his hand. "Starting with this."

Emmett sputtered but didn't put words to his protest as she marched out the door, gingerly holding the cigar between two fingers to show him her distaste.

Defiantly, he went back to the cigar box. But when he lifted the lid, a bit of ecru paper showing at the bottom distracted him.

The letter.

Hesitating only briefly, he picked it out from under the cigars and held it as carefully as he would a snake ready to strike.

He remembered the fury that had filled him when he'd read the damn missive the first time. He'd crumpled it in his fist and had thrown it away. But something had made him retrieve the paper from the waste basket before Felice had a chance to empty it. Something had made him smooth out the wrinkles and save the battered warning, setting it at the bottom of his cigar box because no one but him was allowed to touch the thing.

He hadn't believed the warning, of course. Not right away.

But now, well…the noose was tightening.

Emmett could only hope that he hadn't waited too long.

Chapter Nine

All the way into Taos, Bart's thoughts were filled with Josie Wales.

Who was she? Why did she play so secretive?

Most of all, why did he care?

Taos was an amalgam of cowboy and Pueblo Indian, sophisticated artist and the occasional hippie left over from the seventies. A picturesque tourist mecca, but with a decent number of practical businesses away from the plaza, enough to make the forty-minute trip worth his while.

As he ran his various errands, Bart tried to make sense of his interest in the mysterious woman.

That he was attracted to Josie was a given. That she was in some kind of trouble was equally obvious—it just wasn't in his nature to ignore trouble if he could do something about it. That he might be reading more into the situation than warranted his worry was a distinct possibility.

And yet he couldn't stop himself.

A few hours later, the back of his four-by-four filled with supplies and groceries, Bart picked up Lainey's processed film and decided to grab a fast lunch before heading back to the ranch. He chose a café just off the plaza. While waiting on his burger and fries, he took a look at his daughter's latest photographs and was startled when he came to several of Josie working with the horses.

But the one that made him stop and think was a full head-on shot, closer than the others. Josie's features were crystal-clear, recognizable to anyone who'd ever seen her before.

It didn't take him long to decide.

After gulping down his food without even tasting it, Bart set off to see an old friend in the Taos County Sheriff's Department.

Sheriff John Malone hadn't changed much since Bart had worked with him years before, when he'd started his law enforcement career. A big man, Malone still had a hearty handshake and a killer smile beneath the familiar thick mustache. He suggested they grab some coffee in the back room where they had the place to themselves.

"A rancher." Malone shook his head as he poured two cups. "I don't know. You can take a lawman out of the force, but you can't take the instinct out of the lawman."

"Sounds like you've been talking to Pa. He wants me to run Silver Springs, as well as the Curly-Q."

"Not a bad idea. You can keep your hand in. Think about it. Maybe we can work out something. I'd have you work for me any day."

"I'm flattered." Bart took the cup Malone offered him. "I'm afraid my hands are going to be full as it is. My brothers haven't shown and I don't know if they will. The ranch is on shaky ground, and I'm afraid that no matter how hard I try, we might still lose it."

"That's tough to face. Too many ranches have gone under already." Opposite Bart, Malone twirled a chair around and straddled the seat. "But I don't expect you stopped by to ask my advice about cattle. So what's going on?"

"Actually, I was hoping you could do me a favor." From his shirt pocket, Bart pulled the photo of Josie. "Take a look at this. All I'm trying to do is ID her. *Unofficially.*"

"Long story short?"

"She's working for me and I'm pretty sure she's in some kind of trouble." To Malone's quizzical expression, he added, "She's not talking—and wouldn't explain if I asked her direct. She'd find a way to dance around the subject." He took a slug of the coffee. "She calls herself Josie Wales."

Malone laughed. "Like in the Eastwood movie? The Outlaw Josie Wales?"

"Yeah." *Outlaw...* Bart's gut clenched. "Like the movie."

"So it's an alias."

"I wouldn't bet against it. I doubt she made it very far from where she started out. No vehicle. No money. And I'm pretty sure she was hurt sometime recently."

Malone nodded. "I'll show the photo to the boys around here. And I can fax it to my contacts in other departments around this area of the state, if you want."

"Low profile."

"You bet. But I will make sure to tell them it's a favor for one of their own."

In Bart's heart, he still was. "I owe you, Malone."

The grin reappeared below the mustache. "And one of these days, I might even collect now that you're in the neighborhood, hopefully for good."

Bart started off for home feeling more in control now that he'd decided to act on his gut instinct. But letting someone else do all the leg work didn't sit well with him. He was like Pa in that way.

Outlaw...was she?

REBA'S CAFÉ was owned and operated by a middle-aged woman filled with good humor and draped in flowing garb as colorful as the turquoise-splashed adobe walls and purple trim. The place was cozy and cheerful if not fancy. Josie watched the smiling owner drift from booth to table, making sure her patrons had everything they needed.

Every table and nearly every space at the counter was taken up at the supper hour—mostly men, hired hands with no woman to cook for them—so when the door chimes sang out, the cheerful noise pulled Josie's attention to the entrance.

In walked Hugh Ruskin.

Every inch the predator, he slowly swept his gaze over the room. Until it hit Josie. Those nearly colorless, reptilian eyes swept from her to her companion and back to her where they bored in and held fast. For a moment, the rush of her hastened heartbeat filled Josie's ears. And then the owner rushed to greet him, and Ruskin threw back his head in what Josie could only think of as silent amusement, his white buzz cut fairly bristling with mirth.

Unnerved, she focused on her dinner plate.

Intent on his steak, Bart didn't seem to notice.

She sat across from him in a booth set along the

wall opposite the door. He'd insisted on taking her
to Reba's for dinner. He'd wanted a steak, he'd told
her while driving her back to Alcina's—something
forbidden in Felice's kitchen at the moment because
of his father's heart condition—and he'd wanted
company. Hers. Hence the invitation that she absolutely could not turn down. *His* words.

A famished Josie had quickly accepted with the
provision that she be allowed a quick shower and a
change of clothes. So far, she wasn't sorry, but she
knew she was going to have to keep up her guard
with Bart.

And now she had Hugh Ruskin to worry about.
But when she glanced back across the room, she saw
him sitting at the counter, his back to her.

Relieved, she chowed down some more of her
thick pork chop, home fries, pinto beans and warm
flour tortilla.

Swallowing a mouthful, she asked Bart, "So
what's the plan for tomorrow?"

"More of the same—moving cows so we can get
them to the corrals where we can separate off the
calves." Bart cut a big chunk from what was left of
his steak. "Considering the size of our herd, it'll be
a time-consuming process."

Josie watched the steak disappear into his mouth.
She'd been spending an inordinate amount of time
sneaking looks at the mouth that had kissed her, she
realized. Lips so seductive she wanted to feel them
again. Blushing at the thought, at the way it made
her squirm inside, she was desperate to keep the
conversation on work.

Remembering he'd mentioned the possibility of

hiring a couple of day workers, she asked, "Were you able to get more hands?"

"Yeah—you and me."

A thrill shot through her at the new challenge, but, confident that she'd manage somehow, Josie nodded. "The horses are ready and eager to work and so am I."

"Good. My trust in you is well-deserved, then."

She shifted uncomfortably under his steady gaze. "Trust is important," she mumbled, "especially for a lawman, I guess."

Which made her wonder how far he really did trust her...or would trust her if he knew about the stolen truck.

That thought reminded her of the driver's license she was supposed to produce.

"It's not the occupation that made me the way I am," Bart was saying. "Life did that...along with Pa's help."

"What do you mean?"

"He always operated under his own agenda. Nothing wrong with that if you're up-front with your intentions. But he enjoyed manipulation—situations or people, it was all the same to him as long as he got what he wanted in the end. When I decided I'd had enough, I left."

"That's understandable, but you were bound to leave, anyway, right? To live your own life."

"I'll never be sure of that."

Bart Quarrels not sure of something? Now, that surprised her.

She glanced back toward Ruskin. She could see his reflection in the window. He seemed to be staring at something dead-on in the plate glass. Her?

Even with his back turned, could he be watching her?

Suppressing a shiver, Josie determined to ignore the man.

"Bart, think about this," she said. "If you hadn't left, you wouldn't have met your wife, so something good came of your striking out on your own."

"A lot of good. And I have two great kids to remind me." Bart's words, so rich with pride, made Josie smile. Then his tone shifted to something sad and dark when he went on. "But if Sara had trusted me, everything would be different now."

Her smile faltered. "I—I don't understand."

"She'd be alive."

That gave her pause. Had his wife been in some kind of trouble?

"What happened?"

"Sara had a big heart, especially when it came to kids. She hated that they didn't all have safe homes and loving parents and enough to eat like Daniel and Lainey did. She started working with an organization that helped runaways—an organization that showed more care for the kids than for the law."

Josie recognized the pain in Bart's eyes as going so deep it had to sear his soul. She reached out and touched his hand, ready to whip it back if necessary. But he didn't so much as twitch.

She told him, "You don't have to talk about it."

"I want to." Those penetrating eyes met hers, as if conveying some message he wanted her to understand. His free hand covered hers, binding them together. "God only knows why she didn't tell me what was going on. It's not like I didn't already know the success of the program was in making sure the kids got to shelters where they'd have a bed and food."

"And in keeping the locations of those shelters secret," Josie murmured, too aware of his touch. "Even from the authorities."

She was too aware, and he didn't seem to notice that he was drawing designs on the back of her hand with the tips of his long fingers. She was melting inside—the short, light strokes stoking a fire in her. What started as tickling warmth quickly grew more intense. She had to force herself to focus on what he was saying.

"I didn't know the rest until after. It seemed that one of the fathers somehow learned that Sara was a volunteer, helping to shelter his runaway child from him. This guy was a sicko—sexually obsessed with his fifteen-year-old daughter. He tried to get information about the girl's whereabouts from Sara, but she wouldn't tell him anything, so he started following her. And then threatening her."

His wife in danger because she'd been trying to protect someone...a girl who couldn't protect herself. "How awful," Josie murmured.

She closed her eyes. Mistake. In her mind, that disembodied hand flashed toward her face again. She flashed her eyes open to obliterate the image. Heart thudding, she immediately glanced over at the counter, her instincts to seek out Ruskin.

His stool was empty. A quick glance around the room assured her the bartender was gone. Now, why didn't that make her feel better?

She looked back to Bart, tried to keep her gaze and voice moderated when she wasn't feeling at all normal. Her world had just turned cockeyed and she wasn't sure why.

"Why didn't Sara tell you about this creep?" she asked. "Surely your own wife trusted you."

"Obviously not enough to believe I could handle the situation to her satisfaction."

"Maybe she was afraid you'd turn the girl over to the child welfare people."

Which would have been the legally correct thing to do if not the right thing for an abused girl, who was trying her best to be invisible, Josie thought.

"I've wondered about that," Bart admitted. "I figure she thought that, if I got involved, my duty would be more important to me than this poor girl. No doubt she feared that I would do something to lose the trust of the rest of the kids who depended on having that safe place to turn to."

"And there was always the possibility that the father might have gotten his hands on the girl again once Child Welfare was involved," Josie added.

Her mouth went dry with her increasing distress.

What *would* Bart have done? she wondered.

He might have convinced himself that he wouldn't have let down a woman he was committed to…but he'd also committed himself to uphold the law.

She said, "Unfortunately, the law doesn't always protect the innocent the way it should."

Somehow, Josie knew that fact so intimately that it terrified her.

"I wouldn't have betrayed Sara that way, Josie," Bart insisted. "I would have figured out something…if only she'd trusted me…."

The hurt wasn't fresh anymore, but she could still hear it. Hurt and the guilt.

"So *he* killed her?" she asked. "The father?"

"He finally lost it," Bart agreed. "When Sara refused to tell the bastard his daughter's whereabouts, he shot her. In front of witnesses yet. Then, when he realized what he'd done—and knowing he wasn't going to get away with it—he turned the gun on himself. Both DOA."

Josie's eyes welled with tears. "My God, how tragic. I'm so sorry."

"I can't stop blaming myself."

"But you didn't even know."

"That's the thing. My own wife didn't tell me she was in a dangerous situation and needed some help. That had to be my fault. I must have done something to convince her that she couldn't trust me." His gaze caught hers once more. "I would have helped her," he said solemnly. "Just like I'll help *you* if you'll let me."

The significance of that statement didn't hit her immediately. Then the meaning of his words seeped inside her, sneaking under her skin, filling her with disappointment and anger.

A chill followed, spreading all the way to her hand still wedged between his. Any warmth or connection she'd felt mere moments ago had vanished.

Josie pulled her hand free. "I don't believe this— you set me up!"

Bart shook his head. "I'm just offering—"

"You're not offering anything," she said, cutting him off. "You're just trying to manipulate me."

"What?"

"Just as you accused your pa of doing. I wouldn't

get on my high horse there, if I were you, boss. You're just like him!''

"How?" He sounded outraged.

"You tell me some sad story in hopes that I'll pour out my soul to you."

Though Bart didn't deny that, he said, "Everything I told you is God's truth."

Not wanting to hear more, she whipped out of the booth, thankful that she hadn't let him suck her in any further than he had.

"Take what I owe you for dinner out of my pay! You can drop the rest off at Alcina's."

"You're not quitting."

In response, she gave him her back and fled across the room, dancing around Reba, who was seeing to some customers and blocking her way to the exit.

"Josie, wait a minute!"

Now every eye in the place was on her, as if the café's patrons were watching some show.

"Let's talk about this!" he yelled after her.

At the door, Josie whirled around to face him one last time. He was standing up near the booth, glaring at her, looking for all the world like the injured party. Her sense of outrage intensified.

"Don't you get it?" she asked. "I have nothing to say to you!"

Then she slammed out of the café and stumbled into the street. She hesitated long enough to get her bearings. The moon had sheltered behind a bank of clouds, and, as usual, she had trouble with her night vision. Her eyes couldn't adjust to this little light. But she headed in the general direction of the bed-and-breakfast, anyway, believing instinct would see her home.

A wind swept up the street, sneaking into every entry her clothes allowed. Josie wrapped her arms around her middle, cradling her still-sore rib cage, and tried to think warm.

Disappointment threatened to overwhelm her. She hadn't been prepared for this. She'd known Bart was trouble, certainly, but he was a lawman. She'd trusted him to be a straight shooter. Up-front. She hadn't thought he'd try to use her emotions to trick her into telling him what he wanted to know. Probably the only ploy that could have surprised her.

What a fool she was!

Bart had sucked her in good and she'd followed him every inch of the way. Then he'd been a little too anxious to reveal his hand. He hadn't played her smart, waited until she'd been in too far to get back out.

The thought jarred something loose from the past.

Warm breath feathered the back of her neck, but she was cold inside.

"You need me, honey, 'cause I'm all you got. All you'll ever have. It's time you learned that."

No, she didn't *need him anymore, and she certainly didn't trust him....*

Josie faltered, caught at a porch post and hung on, swaying at the memory that obviously had been instigated by the scene with Bart. The wind licked her with cold so that she started to shake inside.

He was in back of her, arms around her middle. She stood there, frozen, heart pounding, wishing him away. But no matter how hard she wished, he was always there, waiting for his chance.

Her fault she hadn't been smarter in the first place.

Now she had trouble she couldn't even shake with the help of the law....

Another man had wanted her to trust him and she foolishly had, Josie realized. Who was he? And what had spoiled that trust between them? What had that man done to her that she'd been so afraid of him?

An open hand swung toward her....

In a daze, mind searching for the truth, Josie pushed away from the post and careered toward the bed-and-breakfast, moving faster as if she could evade the very truth she sought. The past was catching up to her in more ways than one. And something told her she wasn't really prepared to face it.

She sped by buildings—occupied and abandoned—without focusing. Everything was as much of a blur to her eyes as it was to her mind.

Unable to see where she stepped, Josie stumbled when her toe hit ragged pavement. Even as she caught herself, a hand snagged her waist as if to steady her.

Bart! "Let go—"

But he whipped her around and pulled her between two abandoned buildings.

As Josie slammed against the weathered boards, the breath was knocked out of her. Her entire body sang out with various shades of pain, her side especially, and she realized her mistake. She didn't have to see the glow of his white buzz cut to know this wasn't her lawman.

After leaving the café, Hugh Ruskin must have been waiting for the opportunity to get to her.

The moon had slipped out of its cloud shelter and now beamed silver across the man's cruel expression. He was so close, Josie felt as if she couldn't breathe. His big body nearly touched hers, and his palms rested flat against the wall on either side of her face.

She wanted to move, but she felt frozen with fear.

"So you think you're too good for the likes of me, do you?" he said in a singsong voice.

Josie told herself to keep calm. "I never said that." And told herself to look for an opportunity to make her break.

"Just because I'm a bartender, you think I'm beneath you?" Ruskin asked. "But the boss, he's good enough, right?" His voice lowered to a growl. "Getting into your jeans has to be his only interest—you got nothing else going for you. So what makes you so hot, huh?"

Finding her courage, Josie dodged to her right, but the man caught her and pinned an arm across her throat.

"Nothing," she choked out, anxiety rising. She wanted to fight him, but her muscles all felt locked up. "Let me go, please. Alcina's waiting...."

"I can imagine," Ruskin continued as he dared to run his hand down her belly. "You give him some of this, do you?"

Josie's skin crawled as she felt the path of his fingers through her jeans, and she knew he meant to take what she wasn't willing to give him. Mind whirling, she tried to think of what she could do to hurt him bad. But even as she focused, Ruskin suddenly flew back.

"I warned you not to speak disrespectfully of a lady in my presence!"

Her eyes finally adjusting to the moonlight, Josie saw Bart's fist connect with Ruskin's jaw. The bartender stumbled back, caught himself and rushed in for more. As big as Bart was, Ruskin was bigger. Josie gasped as the two men flew out to the street together.

Fearing Ruskin had the upper hand because of his size, that he would hurt Bart, Josie looked around frantically for a weapon. A couple of boards lay on the ground near the building. Grabbing one, she advanced on the men who were rolling and pounding at each other.

They were like one big knot, arms and legs tangled. A moving knot, no clear shot.

"C'mon," she whispered.

Ruskin lifted himself over Bart and raised his arm with a closed fist.

"Gotcha!" she yelled.

They swung together—her board, Ruskin's fist. Somehow, the mass on the ground shifted and flipped.

A thunk melded with a groan of pain.

"Oh, God!" Josie cried.

She'd hit the wrong man!

Chapter Ten

Ruskin pried himself loose from the tangle, stood and kicked Bart in the ribs for good measure, then stomped off muttering, "You're gonna be real sorry you messed with me!"

A horrified Josie threw down the board and dropped to her knees next to a groaning Bart, who now lay on his side, blood dribbling from his lip.

"Bart! Are you all right?"

"Just dandy."

"Let me give you a hand."

"Uh, no thanks." He rose to one elbow. "You've been help enough for one day."

When Josie made an attempt, anyway, trying to assist him by bracing his arm, his groans convinced her she was merely making his pain worse. "I'm sorry." Guilt at having hit him so hard flooded her.

Imagining she could feel his pain as he rose to a sitting position, Josie said, "You need a doctor."

It took all her will not to touch his poor face. In addition to the bloody lip, she could make out a raw-looking spot high on his left cheek where Ruskin's fist must have made contact.

"Nothing is broken," Bart assured her.

"You can hardly move."

He disproved that by stumbling to his feet. "I'm moving just fine."

But the arm she'd smacked with the board wasn't. Bart was cradling it at his side.

"At least let's take a look at the damage where there's some light before you drive all the way back to the Curly-Q." If it looked bad enough, she'd force him to see a doctor if she had to rope him up and drive him all the way to the nearest real city to find one. "We're almost to Alcina's."

Bart nodded. "As long as you don't try to touch me until we get there."

Tempted to protest, Josie kept her mouth shut. He was hurt because of her. Because he'd tried to help her, even as he'd offered in the café. Here was one man who wasn't all words.

As if he could read her mind, Bart said, "About our altercation at Reba's—I only want to do right by you, Josie. I only want to help you."

If she hadn't believed him before, she did now. Nevertheless, she wasn't going to open up—not when the truth about her having stolen that truck would change the way he looked at her.

"I appreciate your offer," she said, "but I don't need a rescuer."

"Ruskin contradicted that in a big way."

She shuddered. "He's a jerk with more hormones than brains. He could have picked on any woman."

"But he picked on you. And I suspect it had to do with more than hormones. Any idea of what?"

That set up a flurry of questions in her mind. Hugh Ruskin? Could it be? Had she known him before? Was he the kind of man who would ambush a woman with a rifle?

As vile a person as he might be, Josie didn't think that was Ruskin's style. He was open. Liked an audience when he could have one. Probably had enjoyed the altercation with Bart.

When they were in sight of the Silver Springs Bed-and-Breakfast, she said, "Let's go around back."

Josie took Bart inside through the mudroom. The kitchen light was on, so she called, "Anyone here?" but got no response. "This way."

She led him to her narrow room where Miss Kitty waited for her, dancing on tiptoes. Josie picked up the cat, fluffed and hugged her until she purred loudly.

"Take your shirt off," she told Bart, "while I get some towels and ice."

She set the cat on the bed and started to leave until Bart said, "I don't know...I may need *your* help...with these buttons."

His tone was at once vulnerable...and self-mocking. Warmth flushed her, but Josie put up her best front as she stood before him and tried to unhook the button at his neck. Her fingers felt stiff, and she fumbled with it for a moment before getting the button through the hole.

"At this rate, we'll be here all night," he said, his gaze doing funny things to her insides. "Not that I'm complaining."

Flushed through and through, Josie made quick work of the rest. Only when she got to the last button did she realize he probably could have done this himself if he'd tried—both of his arms weren't hurt, after all. But when she got a glimpse of the new bruise starting to bloom across his ribs, chastising him flew from her mind.

"That could be nasty if it isn't taken care of right away," she murmured, her forehead furrowing. "Are you sure you won't see a doctor?"

"Bruised but not broken," he assured her. "Why would I want to see some cranky old guy when I can have a lovely young woman to see to my well-being?"

Gritting her teeth at the intimacy of his tone, Josie pulled the shirttails free of his jeans. That involved some touching, more than made her comfortable. His flesh was warm and seductive wherever she made contact.

"Talk to me, Josie, please," he murmured as she drew closer to him. "Tell me who you're running from."

"I don't know...I mean I'm not..." They were so close that she was almost in his arms. "You're trying to confuse me again."

More touching was involved as she peeled the shirt down off his shoulders, first to free his good right arm, then to slip it off his injured left. Though she tried not to stare, she couldn't help admiring his magnificent musculature, due, no doubt, to countless hours of hard work. Nor could she ignore his flat stomach and the light dusting of hair that trailed down below the waist of his jeans.

Her breath shuddered through her and her teeth tugged at her lower lip as her imagination soared. Then she looked again at his ribs and at his upper arm—the flesh looked angry and swollen where she'd whacked it with the board.

"Go ahead and sit," she said. "I'll get some ice packs."

He didn't move. He cupped her cheek, turned her face to his. "Someone hurt you," he said, his thoughts obviously one-track. "A man. Josie, tell me."

Chest tightening, resisting the seduction of his voice, she pulled away. "I'll be right back."

In the kitchen, the back of her neck prickled...almost as if someone were watching her. The dining room was dark. Flipping on the light revealed nothing out of place. And yet she felt unsettled. She looked out the windows, both kitchen and mudroom. Again, nothing.

"What's taking you so long?" Bart called.

"Another minute!"

Shaking away her unease, Josie quickly gathered some thin dish towels and plastic bags, a bowl of ice and another of warm water. When she returned to her room, Bart was sprawled across her bed, back propped against the wall. Miss Kitty lay beside him, one paw possessively over his thigh.

Her mouth went dry at the thought of touching him so intimately.

"I want to try to keep the bruising down." Setting everything on the little dresser, she filled one of the plastic bags with ice, wrapped a towel around it and handed it to him. "Hold this against your ribs."

Bart said nothing as he took the ice pack from her, but his gaze once more spoke volumes. Self-conscious, trying not to weaken, Josie turned away to prepare a second bag.

Suddenly, he asked, "Are you a big Eastwood fan?"

"What?"

"Clint Eastwood." Though his expression was placid, he was staring at her with increased intensity, as if he were probing, searching for a way into her mind. "It didn't come to me right away, but it makes sense. Clint Eastwood used to make Westerns."

"Your arm." She handed him the second ice pack. "I know who Clint Eastwood is."

He wedged the first pack against his ribs with his elbow, then pressed the second pack against his upper arm.

"Is that how you picked your name—from the movie *The Outlaw Josey Wales?*"

Josie sighed. So he knew she'd given him a fake name. Leave it to her to pick one that sounded vaguely familiar and went with the initials on her belt buckle and turned out to be a name from a well-known movie.

Her back to him as she dipped the edge of a towel in the warm water, she hedged, "Don't be ridiculous."

Moving to the bed to clean his face, she had to place one knee on the mattress to get close enough. Miss Kitty had the good sense to jump away before she got in the crush. The cat moved to the other end of the bed where she could watch comfortably from a pillow.

"Then you won't mind showing me your driver's license," Bart continued, watching her closely. "You said it was in your bag." He indicated the corner where she'd left it. "You can get it now, right?"

"No."

Her stomach in knots at the thought of being exposed, Josie placed her free hand under Bart's jaw so that she could tilt his face and clean it. She concentrated on her first aid rather than the question in his eyes, starting with the hot spot high on his cheek. A little scrape, thankfully nothing more, she thought. Then she turned the cloth to a fresh spot and dabbed at the dried blood on his lip. The cut reopened and a bead of blood pooled there.

Josie winced for him.

Before she could turn the cloth and dab again, Bart sat up, which placed the length of his nude torso mere inches from her. Josie couldn't stop the sudden thrumming of her pulse.

"You have a kind heart and a gentle soul," he said. "Animals are never wrong about that, you know. They have good instincts and so do I."

Realizing that he was trying to tell her something in a roundabout way—that he trusted her?—Josie still felt confused as to why that should be so important to her. She lowered her gaze and stared at the cleft in his chin.

Before she fathomed his intention, Bart dropped the ice pack from his arm and hooked his hand behind her neck. Not knowing if it was from the cold or his touch, she shivered. He slowly pulled her head toward him. Then he brushed her mouth with his. Just a momentary touch. Even so, she shuddered at the sensation that was strangely erotic.

"So…what is your name?"

The salty metallic taste of his blood lingered on her lower lip, reminding her once more of her guilt.

"Josie Wales."

That guilt edged her response. Bart had come to

her rescue more than once. He'd proved himself to be someone she could count on. But could she trust him to stand behind her if she told him everything? Rather, all she'd remembered or conjectured to date, which wasn't much.

His lips trailed along her cheek to her ear where he whispered, "Your *real* name."

If only she knew…

Hot tears sprang to the backs of her eyelids.

He kissed her again. Deeper…sweeter…longer. His mouth lingered over hers for a moment. She savored every second.

And then he released her mouth, asking, "Why won't you tell me?"

The moment of truth. Could she do it? How long could she avoid it? Besides, she was tired of being strong. Alone. Her burden was so heavy, she could use a shoulder to lean on. A shoulder belonging to someone who cared for her.

But…did he?

Unable to stand another evasion…call it what it was, a lie…she finally let it go.

"I can't tell you anything different, because I don't know!"

"C'mon, trust me."

Could she? How could she be certain he wasn't just trying to manipulate her as she'd suspected him of doing all along at the café?

Josie pushed Bart away from her and tried to ignore the way he sucked in air. But his pain was *her* pain, if only for a moment. She couldn't forget he'd just stopped something unpleasant from happening to her.

"I *don't* know," she insisted, "because I don't remember!"

Bart arched one eyebrow at her. "Now, who's trying to play whom?" he asked softly.

In for a penny…

"I was in an accident," she explained. "The truck I was driving went off the highway."

Certain he'd have his ways of checking things out for himself, Josie didn't say the word *stolen*. She couldn't brand herself a thief in his eyes. Not yet. He'd own the whole truth soon enough.

"I woke up not knowing who I was," she continued. "Not remembering anything about the accident…or anything that happened to me before the accident, for that matter."

"Amnesia. You're serious?"

"Afraid so."

"How long?"

"The day before we met, actually."

"And nothing has come back to you?"

"Only wisps of memory. Nothing substantial…yet."

How could she tell Bart that she remembered some faceless, nameless man hitting her…that she relived her own sense of feeling trapped and scared…that she imagined that same man was here in Silver Springs stalking her?

Though she expected more questions in the same vein from him, they didn't come. Truth be told, she didn't know if she was relieved…or disappointed.

"So, you have a life out there somewhere you don't remember," he said. "And a family."

"No family—"

"I thought you didn't remember."

"I don't." Was he trying to trick her? "I just…know." Unable to explain her certainty, she shrugged her shoulders.

When Bart sank into a thoughtful silence, Josie immediately grew uneasy. He was distancing himself from her. She could sense it.

That trust thing went two ways, she thought, as her stomach churned. Bart wanted her to trust him…but he obviously didn't trust her.

If he cared, he would take her into his arms to reassure her. But that seemed like the furthest thing from his mind right now. Then, again, he'd never said he cared and why should he? He didn't even know her. Attraction didn't equal commitment, especially when he had no idea of what she might be getting him into.

Josie backed away and slipped off the bed, catching Miss Kitty in her arms to anchor herself. She didn't want to think about this anymore. Didn't want to examine her own feelings. The cat gave her an adoring look, then settled against her chest and purred.

A seemingly reluctant but obviously determined Bart rose, as well. He grabbed his shirt and carefully slipped the injured arm into the sleeve.

"So that bag of yours," he said, "has no clues as to your identity?"

"Only…" She'd started to tell him about the pin, but why? It wouldn't tell him who she was, and that seemed to be the only thing important to him. "I only wish," she said instead. She searched his face as he fumbled with the buttons. Did he believe her or not? Did he trust her? She thought not. "I take it you're leaving."

Hands suddenly motionless, he gave her one of those penetrating looks. "Is that an invitation to stay?"

She wanted him to stay, Josie realized. Wanted him to hold her in his arms all night. Wanted him to make her feel safe. Wanted…more…something she wasn't willing to put words to…not now.

What she said was, "I—I just thought you might need to recuperate for a while longer."

"I'll just get stiff."

He suddenly *sounded* stiff, she thought. "But you've hardly used the ice packs—"

"Not a problem. We have an ice-maker at the ranch. And a hot tub."

Josie hated the way he suddenly sounded so…neutral. Excuses. He wanted to get away from her, was all. Maybe he thought that she was lying about the amnesia. Or that she was merely unstable. He was wearing a poker face, so she didn't have a clue.

"Bart, what are you going to do exactly?" she asked, pulse threading unevenly, this time from some fear she couldn't define. "About me, I mean?"

"I thought you didn't need rescuing."

"I—I don't. I just thought…nothing."

She wasn't fooled by his manner. He would do what came naturally to a lawman, of course. He would investigate her. He would learn she was a thief, and then he would fire her.

Or worse, he might have her arrested.

Her stomach burned at the thought.

Tim Harrigan's offer to take her anywhere away

from here was sounding far more tempting than when he'd proposed it.

If only she had someplace to go...

JOSIE STILL WASN'T BEING straight with him.

The certainty plagued Bart as he drove back to the ranch. She was hiding something. The reason someone would have to shoot at her?

An accident. Amnesia. It all fit.

Sore ribs—if not caused by a fist, he thought grimly—could be the downside of wearing a seat belt. And while the bruise had faded to nothing now, the side of her face could have been injured smacking into the window in a crash.

A head injury would explain it.

How bad would the injury have to be to wipe out a person's long-term memory as well as the short? And for so long—judging from the fast-fading bruises, a week or so. He'd heard of cases of hysterical amnesia, of course, in which psychological rather than physical trauma was the cause. Had something so terrible happened to Josie that she'd wiped it clear out of her mind?

Bart's head buzzed with anger at the possibility of another woman he cared about being in danger.

A woman he cared about...

He did, Bart realized, amazed, because he'd only known Josie for a few days. He'd dated Sara for weeks before he'd realized his feelings for her ran deeper than friendship. And Josie was so different from his late wife.

Could he be responding to the danger she was in? Trying to save Josie because he hadn't been able to save his wife? Confusing those emotions with something more personal?

The Outlaw Josey Wales…a woman on the run. From what?

Outlaw…

He shook that thought away faster than it came to him. But it sat there in his subconscious until he had to take it back out to examine it.

Could the Josie he knew have been involved in something illegal? Or have been accused of it? Is that why she was running and keeping secrets?

Bart wanted to shake Josie for being so foolish. Sara had kept secrets from him and he'd lost her for it. It all came down to a matter of trust.

Simply put, Josie didn't trust him, and Bart didn't know how to deal with that fact.

Chapter Eleven

Bart was determined to keep his emotional distance the next day when he picked up Josie. But the moment she slid in beside him, he felt his determination waver. Though he knew she could be tough, all his instincts made him want to protect her. A level of commitment that went unappreciated on her part. He wanted to yell at her for being so stubborn. So distrusting of his good intentions.

Instead, he hung on to his temper and said nothing at all. Though he was aware that she sneaked a couple of looks at him, Josie didn't say a word, either, so they drove the first few miles in a silence heavy with tension.

Bart didn't realize how heavy until Josie asked, "How's your arm doing?" and he realized he had a stranglehold on the steering wheel.

Relaxing some, he said, "A little sore is all."

"Good. Not good that it's sore," she quickly amended. "Good that it's not worse. I, uh—" she cleared her throat nervously "—really do appreciate your coming to my rescue last night."

Even knowing how much it took her to say those

particular words, Bart waited for more. When none came, he gave in. "It's the lawman in me, I guess."

"Oh."

He thought she sounded disappointed, so he added, "And as someone who also cares about what happens to you, Josie, I wouldn't have done anything different."

Though he'd bite off his tongue before asking her to trust him again.

Josie lapsed back into silence, but this time it was more comfortable, like when two people knew each other well and were content just being together.

The way he had been with Sara.

Bart missed that special companionship beyond his missing Sara herself. No one could ever take her place in his heart, he knew, but his heart was big enough for someone else, as well.

When he realized the direction of his thoughts, Bart got a little jittery. Decided conversation was needed to settle him down.

Figuring the ranch was the safest topic, he asked, "Have you picked out a horse for yourself?"

"I'm leaning toward Phantom, the little black with the white blaze and feet. She's got plenty of spunk. I believe she considers herself the boss horse, but she responds to every command I give her."

"And if she gives you trouble, you have those spurs to back you up."

"I'm surprised you noticed."

"If you don't want to be noticed, better remove those jingle bobs," he said.

Making music being the sole purpose of the tiny pear-shaped pendants dangling from the rowel axles.

"I guess Phantom is as good as I can ask for my foray into real cowboying."

Bart glanced over and noticed she was grinning. Her mischievous smile was contagious. It lit up her face, made her look real pretty, he thought, his blood humming.

He grinned back and said, "No doubt you'll be as good as anyone at moving cows."

She narrowed her gaze at him. "That is a compliment, right?"

"Absolutely."

The sky was a clear azure blue, and the October morning was moderately warm with a nice breeze. Perfect for a cattle drive. The weather channel had predicted impending rains that night, though, so he hoped that the drive would go off without a hitch and that the weather held till they got to the upper pasture. Nothing to look forward to about moving cows in the rain, he remembered, as they reached the bottom of the rimrock.

He and his brothers had gotten miserable and short-tempered with one another in bad weather more times than he could count. Once they'd had a free-for-all that had ended in the mud, and Pa had wupped them good, had shamed them just for being boys. At the time, Bart had just turned thirteen, Reed had been ten and Chance had only been six.

They were halfway down to the canyon floor when Bart spotted the loose band of horses ready to gang up on them. As usual, they took seriously their job of challenging the noisy "metal animal" invading their territory.

Josie's asking "So what are the plans for today?" took his attention away from the band.

"We'll all ride out together to move the cattle that the boys brought out from the north pasture yesterday. We need to get them up to the flats. Then we'll be one step closer to shipping them to market."

Thereby getting enough money to cover one of the back mortgage payments. Or so he hoped. Beef prices could change overnight. Even a penny a pound was enough to make a big difference in the take-home with a herd this size. But he didn't have the option of waiting out the market until it turned in their favor.

If he waited, they could lose the ranch.

"How many head?" Josie asked.

"Nearly two hundred cows and their calves. The boys already separated off the bulls," he told her. "And once we get these critters in, we'll start moving a herd from another pasture. Then another after that one. Can't do them all at once without more help, that's for sure."

He was going to have to pin down Pa on that one. Either his brothers were going to show, or he was going to have to hire more hands, or the neighbors were going to have to be as willing to pitch in as Pa thought they were. This was one place where Pa could work without putting his health at further jeopardy, Bart decided, and it would give him that "something to do" the old man kept grousing about.

The band of horses jogged alongside them, veering off when they neared the buildings. Bart pulled into the yard and noticed a motorbike alongside the pickups parked in front of the storage shed. Peter Dagget was a local still living with his family, so he hadn't bunked down here for the night.

"Looks like the kid is early this morning."

Josie looked around. "Peter? Where? I don't see him."

Neither did Bart. "Hmm. Maybe he went over to the bunkhouse to chew the fat with the boys."

But when Frank and Will came out ready to work, the men said they hadn't seen the kid. Then the dogs rushed out from the hired man's quarters, with Moon-Eye following.

"I thought I heard a bike around dawn," he said when asked, "but I fell asleep again. I been out and around since, but never saw Peter. Thought maybe Felice invited him inside or something."

Moon-Eye was the only hand who hadn't come over to the main house for a big breakfast. Most mornings, he liked to eat in his own quarters—"the only time a hired hand has to himself to think," he often said.

"I didn't hear anything this morning," Bart admitted. He'd tossed and turned for hours, his mind troubled with thoughts of Josie, before he'd drifted off. And then he must have been sleeping like the dead. "But why would the kid come out here so early?"

No one seemed to have an opinion on that one.

"Where's Juniper?" Josie asked suddenly. "Did you pasture her last night?"

"No," Bart said, scanning the loose horses who were wandering around, picking at the wisps of smashed grass underfoot. "She was still loose when I got home from supper. Ought to be around here somewhere."

Josie shook her head. "I don't see her...oh, no! Hang on."

Taking off like a shot for the tack shed, which sat

alongside the barn, she was inside in a minute. Another minute and she was back out and looking worried.

"One of the saddles is gone!" she cried. "I told Peter he couldn't ride Juniper in no uncertain terms," she said, voice ripe with rising panic. "I told him she's only green-broke."

"If the kid gets dumped," Moon-Eye said darkly, "he asked for his own trouble."

"I'm more worried about his doing something stupid with Juniper. He doesn't have a clue about horses. What if he ruins her as a cattle horse?"

Or worse? Knowing how Josie felt about animals, Bart was certain more dire issues had crossed her mind. He wasn't going to let her go off, half-cocked with worry over the horse.

He held her gaze. "Then, Josie, I trust you to undo whatever it is."

BART QUARRELS HAD SAID he trusted her.

Hours later, as she followed the herd, Josie was still reeling from the admission.

Wearing a pair of borrowed chinks—someone's old "high water" fringed chaps that hit her mid-shin when she stood—Josie was riding drag alongside Moon-Eye, who drove one of the ranch pickups. In his vehicle, he was nearly as effective as anyone on horseback, if not quite as agile. While he kept pushing the herd forward, she was the one who had to bring the stubborn stragglers back in line, a bandanna over her lower face so she wouldn't choke on the dust they kicked up.

Moon-Eye drove with the window open and sans bandanna. She could hear his radio and his off-key singing as red dust floated through his cabin. The best part of his being along was that a big cooler of food—which meant a substantial lunch—was perched on the bed of his pickup.

The herd fanned out ahead of them in a long line, five and six abreast. Frank and Will were the swing riders—keeping crafty cows and their progeny from swinging wide and creating chaos by trying for a different direction. A.C. and D.C. took noisy pleasure in helping the cowboys.

And at the head of the long column, making sure those critters in the lead moved steadily toward the ungraded path cut in the rimrock that would take them up to the flats, Bart rode point.

Bart *trusted* her, she marveled again.

That is, he trusted her to fix any possible problem with Juniper, Josie analyzed, if she took his words at face value only. But the way he'd said it—with the emphasis on *trust*—she was certain he'd put a wealth of meaning behind his simple statement.

Josie was feeling touched and guilty and giddy all at once. Not to mention worried—about Peter and Juniper, that was.

Where had the kid gotten himself to?

It was nearly noon now, and no word. Bart had brought the cell phone along so that Felice could call him if she spotted either teenager or mare.

Josie had meant to ride out looking for them, but Bart had insisted he needed her for the drive. He needed them both, really, and now he'd lost his newest hand for good. She knew Bart would fire Peter the moment he set eyes on the kid.

That something was really wrong either with horse or rider sat heavily on her mind.

They reached the base of the rimrock and Bart pushed the lead cows up the path. Both Frank and Will hung back at the base until most of the herd was on its way up.

They'd made it with time to spare. Only one more gate to drive the herd through and that about a half mile in on the flats. And enough time for that lunch before doing so, she thought, her stomach growling.

She was hanging back, away from the truck, watching the herd's progress, when a set of hoof-beats back the way they'd come alerted her. Standing in the saddle, she turned to see a cloud of red dust, the head of a blue roan enveloped in the swirling center.

"Hey, there's Peter!" she shouted to Moon-Eye.

"I only see the mare!"

As did she, Josie realized, knowing she was going to have to intercept the panicked horse before she did herself some damage. She pressed Phantom to cut off the other mare. But the cloud of dust accompanying the roan was too extensive to be raised by her hooves alone.

Pounding down on the foaming mare, she saw Peter at last, bouncing and flipping along the ground, his right foot somehow still jammed into that stirrup.

"Oh, God!"

She cut directly into Juniper, turning her and catching her dangling reins. It took a moment to slow her. Josie didn't even realize she was holding her breath until she brought both mares to a stop.

"Easy, girl, easy!" she gasped.

Dismounting, she slung both sets of reins around a branch of a nearby cypress and ran her hand along the roan's neck to calm her so she would stay put. Hot, wet flesh shuddered under her palm, but Juniper didn't seem about to spook again.

Her stomach burning, Josie managed to free the boot from the stirrup.

"Peter, are you all right?"

But he didn't answer.

He lay there so still, broken limbs bent like a rag doll's, face and head bloody. She flew to her knees but was afraid to touch him further.

"Peter, please...wake up...say something!"

But Peter Dagget couldn't answer. Not when he was already dead.

JOSIE WAS WHITE AND SHAKING and appeared to be in shock by the time Bart got to her.

All stiff, back straight as a rod, she sat on the ground next to the kid, holding his hand. When Bart got a better look, he winced. Even though he knew, he had to check for a pulse to be sure. His gut constricted as he confirmed it.

Poor kid—not much older than his own son. He couldn't even imagine how to tell the parents....

"I *told* him not to ride Juniper." Josie's gray eyes were watery as they met his, but somehow she managed to hold on. "Why didn't he listen to me?"

"It isn't your fault."

"I should have known he would—"

"You couldn't have known."

"The horses are my responsibility."

"But you're not responsible for this."

Josie swallowed hard and nodded as if she were trying to believe him, but Bart didn't think she was convinced. Feeling sick himself over this unnecessary death, he helped her to her feet. Tempted to take her in his arms to comfort her—and him—he resisted. That might just break her to pieces. He needed her to be strong for a little while longer.

Moon-Eye pulled the old pickup close. Who would have known they'd have more use for the vehicle than to carry some tools and their lunch?

The hired hand limped alongside them, muttering, "Danged fool kid. Neck broken?"

Bart figured as much. Peter's head was a mess— all bloody, indicating it had taken quite a beating. He hunkered down next to the body again and checked it over.

"It's broken."

No matter how many dead bodies he'd seen—and he'd seen quite a few in his dozen years as a deputy—he'd never gotten used to it. But he could approach it professionally, Bart decided, taking a better look.

The kid must have been riding somewhere with a lot of rock. Most of the damage was on the right side of his skull, as if, in flipping off the horse, his head had crashed into a sharp edge of a boulder. His gut constricted again, and he only hoped Josie hadn't gotten too close a look. Unfortunately, he suspected she had.

"Let's get him out of here."

Josie moved in to help.

"Not you," he said gently. "I meant Moon-Eye. The two of us can handle it."

She nodded again, then backed off. But Bart knew she didn't take her eyes off them as he and the hired hand picked up the kid and hauled his lifeless body to the pickup.

He knew she was blaming herself for this death. And he knew what blame felt like. So after they set down the body, he tried to reassure her again.

"This is nobody's fault, Josie. Not even his. Peter might have been a reckless kid, but he wasn't out to kill himself. And Juniper wasn't out to kill him, either. It was a terrible, tragic accident, is all."

His heart went out to her. She appeared numb, in shock, unable to comprehend what had happened here. And this on top of her own problems. Hating that she had to go through this, Bart figured he'd better get her someplace where she could feel safe. When she remained silent, he wondered if she could even get back on her own.

"You want to ride shotgun with Moon-Eye?" he asked, offering her an easy option.

"No. I'll take the horses." Her eyes focused at last and she took a big breath as if she were finally able to take it all in. "Yours, too, if you want."

Bart considered the offer. He'd left Frank and Will with the herd with instructions to keep them moving. They didn't have far to go, but they had a lot of cows to handle. Even though there were only the two of them, he figured they could manage to get the critters through one more gate.

He had to deal with Peter Dagget's death, and at this point, a tired horse would slow him down.

"You can handle three horses?"

"I'm your wrangler, remember."

"All right." Maybe that was best for her.... "I'll go back with Moon-Eye. How about if we leave food—you can bring some up to the boys before heading back for the barn."

He only hoped that wasn't pushing her too hard.

Somehow, though, he thought she needed to stay busy for a while.

"I can handle that."

Bart knew Josie could handle a whole lot more and probably had. But she looked as if she'd been pushed to her limit. As if…one more thing and she would go over the edge.

He only prayed he would be there to catch her if and when she fell.

SOMEHOW, JOSIE WENT through the motions. Leaving Juniper and Arrow tied up, she delivered the food to Frank and Will. Relieved that they didn't ask too many questions, she helped them deliver the herd before going back for the other horses.

Juniper was calm and dry now. No trace of the spooked horse she had been while dragging Peter's body. Even so, the violence of the death stayed with Josie.

Shuddering, she closed her eyes to center herself.

An open hand flashed toward her…contact drove back her head.

Stunned, she was alerted by a nervous whinny. She squinted into the dark recesses of the barn, but poor night vision betrayed her once more. All she could see was the glint off his pale hair, but she sensed he was doing something to Dreamsickle… thought he was pulling on the sorrel's reins.

"Stay away from her!"

"What's mine is mine," he told her with a chilling laugh. *"Get in my way and you'll be sorry.…"*

Josie gasped at the fading memory and concentrated. Tried to bring it back. Tried to see the man's face.

But, in the end, her memory failed her once more.

Even so, she tried forcing her mind to respond all the way back to the barn. An exercise in futility.

She brought the horses in just as the ambulance was leaving with the body. Bart and Moon-Eye met her at the corral gate outside the barn, where she flipped the three sets of reins over a pipe.

Bart said, "I was starting to worry."

"No need. I'm fine."

She wasn't fine—how could she be fine after such a horrible shock?—but she was dealing with it.

"I have to take care of things, talk to Peter's folks," Bart said. "I can drop you off at Alcina's on the way."

So she could sit alone and think? And it was early. Hours and hours to relive the horror in her mind. Exhausted she might be, but Josie knew she wouldn't sleep.

Holding panic at bay by a thin thread, she said, "There's work, right? So let me help Moon-Eye."

"I was gonna go talk to the Daggets with the boss," the hired hand said. "I know the family from way back."

"Then give me something to do," Josie begged, desperate to keep busy. She looked from one man to the other. "Please!"

Moon-Eye said, "I suppose you could take water out to the girls in the northwest pasture—"

But Bart interrupted. "The weather channel talked about rain tonight."

Clouds were starting to gather overhead, but nothing imminent, Josie thought. Nothing threatening.

"The weatherman could be wrong. Besides, the

girls might be thirsty now. So tell me how to get there.''

Moon-Eye looked to Bart, who gave him a go-ahead nod.

After the roundup, Josie had a better picture of the north end of the ranch, so she was able to follow his directions in her mind.

''I don't think I'll have any problem finding it,'' she said, just as Frank rode in alone and dismounted near them.

''Where's Will?'' Bart asked.

''We were missing a few head. He stayed behind to flush them out. What do you want me to do next, boss?''

''Ride fence. That south pasture needs to be checked over. We lost a handful of cows last month, and Pa found some fence down.''

''I'll get me a fresh horse and be right on it.'' Frank led off his mount, saying, ''Hey, boss, I'm real sorry about the kid. You tell his folks that for me, would you?''

''Sure thing.'' Bart looked to Moon-Eye. ''We'd better get a move on.'' Then even as Josie dragged the hose across the yard, he asked, ''Are you sure you want to do this?''

''I might go crazy if I don't.''

Although she might go crazy, anyway, Josie feared, as the men left. She stepped up to the portable tank, which was strapped down to the bed of a rusting pickup, inserted the hose into the opening and turned on the water.

As the tank filled, she took care of the horses she'd brought in. Removing saddles and bridles and turning Phantom and Arrow back into their pasture didn't exactly keep her mind occupied.

"What am I going to do with you?" she asked Juniper softly.

The roan pushed at her like always. Josie stroked the velvet nose. Then she walked over to the cake truck and scooped out a handful of pellets. Even as she offered Juniper the treat, she wondered if she'd ever be able to ride the mare after what had happened.

Not that she was afraid...just freaked.

Josie couldn't help wondering if she shouldn't have done something different—as in befriending the kid and giving him a serious talking-to about handling the horses. Or maybe she should just have kept Juniper out of his reach.

But what if Peter's death hadn't been an accident? a little voice in her head questioned.

What if someone had caused it...having mistaken the skinny teenager for *her?*

Chapter Twelve

A threatening gray sky was pushing down on Silver Springs as Bart pulled his vehicle into the gas station.

Moon-Eye slid out of the passenger side. "I'll take care of it—want to get a few things anyhow."

"Go ahead."

Bart began pumping gas and looking at the sky. He was thinking that the weather wouldn't hold much longer when he noticed Alcina Dale pull in.

Leaving her car, she walked over to him.

"Bart, what are you doing in town so early?" she asked, her smile reflecting her pleasure in seeing him, then her brow wrinkling as she got a better look at his face. But she kept any speculation on his bruised cheek and cut lip to herself. "I expected you would be moving cows until dark."

"Work's over for today—we had a bad accident," he said grimly. "Peter Dagget—a kid I just hired—took out a green-broke horse without permission. Unfortunately, something went terribly wrong."

Alcina made a sound of distress. "I-I'm so sorry. He *is* all right?"

"Afraid not." Bart's visage darkened. "I just had to tell his parents."

Her expression shocked, she said, "Oh, Bart, how terrible for you. Who would ever have thought the Curly-Q would have such bad luck, one on top the other? First Josie, now this."

"Josie!" he snapped. "What about her?"

"The other day—she got thrown, right?"

He freed the nozzle and replaced it in its cradle at the pump. "Is that all she told you?"

Alcina started as if she was torn about something. "About *that* particular incident, yes."

Which raised Bart's deputy antenna.

He asked, "So she told you what else? Anything about last night?"

She echoed, "Last night?"

"After supper. Hugh Ruskin, the new bartender at the Silver Slipper was waiting for Josie when she was on her way back to your place—"

"Alone?"

"—and he attacked her."

"That explains your face...but, Bart Quarrels, what were you thinking, letting Josie walk home alone after dark?" Alcina demanded.

"She's a woman with a mind of her own!"

"But if he *is* here, then she may be in real danger—"

"He, who?"

Alcina tightened her lips and gave him a stare that undoubtedly would shrivel a lesser man.

"Alcina...!"

"All right. Josie thinks he's here—some man from her past."

"And she remembers him?" he asked, voice tight.

"She told you about the amnesia? Thank goodness." She shook her head. "No, she doesn't remember him, but she does remember being afraid...of him hitting her."

Bart let out an expletive that reflected his opinion of a man who would raise a hand to a woman.

"I've been picking up on things, too," he said. "Like she always seems to be looking over her shoulder. Did she tell you anything else?"

"No, but our paths really haven't crossed much in the past few days," Alcina said.

A movement caught Bart's attention and he noticed Moon-Eye coming out of the station eating a candy bar.

"I'm glad you know now, though," Alcina was saying. "So you can look out for her. This man...I think he's dangerous, Bart. She was set to run again...to try to lose him. I hope I did the right thing by talking her into staying."

"You did the right thing," he assured her. "Josie doesn't have to run, not from anyone, not ever again. I'm going to see to it."

Alcina breathed a sigh of relief even as Moon-Eye caught up to them.

"Hey, boss, we'd better get back, huh?" He indicated the sky.

Bart nodded curtly. "We'll talk again. Thanks, Alcina."

He only hoped he *could* protect the woman whose past might catch up to her at any moment.

THUNDER RUMBLED in the distance as Josie drove the pickup for the barn. The cows had been glad for the water she'd hauled, but Bart had been right about the rains coming. Still the trip out hadn't been a waste as far as she was concerned. She'd needed work—even busy work—to keep her on an even keel.

Even so, Peter Dagget's death haunted her.

What if it hadn't been an accident?

Fog fingering, the old pickup raised her hackles, and a weird feeling shot through her.

Josie hated driving in bad weather, and this particular drive was worse than most. The rock highway with teeth-clacking, back-breaking drops was a piece of cake compared to the bridge. Rusting old cables that supported rotting boards were suspended over Silverado Creek. The too-narrow bridge swaying as she inched across it had been one thing, but the breaking boards beneath her tires had been quite another, enough to scare anyone, she thought. She wondered if Bart knew what bad repair the bridge was in—he'd surely do something about it when she told him.

As if he didn't have enough to deal with already, she thought, feeling Peter Dagget's lifeless hand in hers once more.

That set her to thinking about it again.

What if the lanky kid had been mistaken for her?

A very real possibility…who else should have been working with the green-broke horse but her?

The first fat raindrops hit the windshield. She turned on the lights and started the wipers.

Clack-clack…clack-clack…clack-clack…

The ragged sound dug deep inside, battering her. Josie tried to shake away the weird feeling, but before she knew what was happening, she lost her focus.

She held her breath, the only sounds filling her ears the rumble of the engine punctuated by worn wipers clack-clacking as they streaked across the windshield....

Her heart beating in time with the wipers, Josie snapped out of the memory as fast as she'd whirled into it.

The accident. Had to be! She'd been driving a pickup as old as the one she was driving now. The night had been as threatening as this, too. A threat. *Him.* The one who roused such fear in her.

The certainty that the man from her past had undoubtedly followed her from the hospital was stronger than ever.

But who was he?

Other than Bart, only three men were possibilities. He had to be one of them, but which? It was her responsibility to figure it out.

She focused on the accident...hoped for some clue...let her mind float...

She would never be free of him. She'd tried everything, and still he was there, a dark phantom, a portent of her future.

He would never let her go. Never let her get away. Never let her live...

Josie gasped. Had he been trying to kill her? But why? What had she done?

Surely nothing as simple as rejecting him.

Hugh Ruskin hadn't taken her rejection well. Could she have known him before? Could she have responded in any way to such a crude man?

Will "Billy Boy" Spencer knew her. How well?

He'd been playing verbal games with her, but he hadn't pressed her.

And what about Tim Harrigan, the loner who'd lost everything, yet volunteered to give time and even money to her in the guise of a kindred spirit?

"Think," she muttered. "Which one?"

Which of her three suspects would have been on the ranch early enough to see Juniper with a rider that he assumed was her? Only Will. But was Billy Boy the murdering type? Josie couldn't fathom it. Neither could she put the thought away.

Back to the accident...

She had no one to blame but herself.

Sickness welled in her as she acknowledged what she had brought down on herself...the bitter taste of acid filled her mouth....

Her stomach tightened and the now-familiar burning began. But her stress was two-fold—the face she was trying to remember and the sight before her she couldn't avoid. There was no helping it—she had to cross the bridge. It lay before her enveloped in arms of fog and drizzle. She could barely make it out.

Pulse thrumming, stomach churning, Josie approached cautiously, going no faster than her headlights would allow her to see ahead....

Her eyes filled again, this time with bright, blinding lights. The windshield wipers swept the image into focus: an eighteen-wheeler, horn blaring....

Coming to with a jerk of the wheel, Josie heard the first crunch. More rotted planks breaking. She feared going on, feared stopping.

She was tired of being afraid.

But there was no helping it, not this time, not when a maw of blackness lay in the path of her headlights—a bunch of boards simply missing as if someone had removed them.

"Oh, my God!"

Stomping on the brake, Josie tried to stop, but the pickup was slow in responding. It rolled right to the edge of the hole and kept moving. Then the front end pitched forward.

Flying without wings, for a second, suspended...

Suddenly, a roller-coaster drop whipped her head into the side window and churned her stomach into her throat. Then the upended truck careered downward.

Flaxen mane...almond-shaped blue eyes...a fresh grave... Clack-clack...clack-clack...clack-clack...

BART CLOSED THE SNAP at the base of his throat and hunkered down into his rubber slicker. The rain had gotten serious. Every time he bent his head, water streamed from his hat brim.

He barely tightened his legs against his mount's sides and Honcho moved out. He'd chosen to ride a big sorrel gelding, who hadn't been worked yet. Despite the rain, the horse was anxious to go and would have endurance, if needed.

Though he was probably worrying for nothing.

Bart tried telling himself that he would run into Josie any minute now. Only he didn't, and the farther he got from the house, the more worry ate at him.

He'd suspected something was wrong when he'd returned from town and Josie hadn't been waiting. Not knowing what he might face in this weather, he'd chosen to go after her on horseback. Often in country like this, an animal could go where a vehicle couldn't.

They were jogging along the creek trail and the bridge wasn't too far ahead—not that he could see it through weather like pea soup. Still no Josie. Knowing Honcho would go berserk if asked to cross something so rickety, Bart wove his way down to the water's edge. The incline was steep and slick, and they went down with the horse's haunches practically sitting in the muck. Luckily, Bart found a narrow spot in the creek where they could cross without too much difficulty.

Even so, the rushing water had already risen nearly a foot, leaving Bart wondering how much higher it would be on the return trip, a problem since no alternate route existed.

Rising water was always something to be concerned about in this country, but no more than Josie herself. That talk with Alcina had set Bart to some wild speculations.

Now he was wondering if there was more to Peter's death than he'd originally suspected. If Josie's mystery man were somehow involved.

Hard to believe the death hadn't been an accident, though. Juniper had come from the direction of the Silver Springs Mine. That pasture was really rocky in spots—that accounted for the damage to the kid's head and all the blood. No herd grazed there because the cows had been moved from the pasture after the anthrax outbreak, so it was a smart place for someone to hide out.

Generally no one went there, Bart thought, so why had the kid?

That train of thought ended the moment a horn

blasted. A startled Honcho jogged to the side and snorted.

"What the—" Bart muttered, quickly bringing the horse under control.

The horn kept blaring and Bart goosed the gelding forward toward the source of the noise.

The bridge lay just ahead, and finally Bart could see it. Mere yards from the bank, twin beams—headlights—cut through the fog and rain, illuminating the vehicle precariously suspended, half-on, half-off the bridge.

The horn blasted again and Bart recognized the pattern—the same pattern Josie used to whistle for the horses.

"Josie!" he yelled, his gut tightening. "Hang on! I'm coming!"

All kinds of thoughts raced through Bart's mind as he moved in on the accident waiting to happen.

An accident that could prove fatal to the woman who was already a part of his heart.

A VOICE CUT THROUGH the fog between horn blasts. Carefully, Josie rolled down the window.

"Josie!" She heard her name even as she was deluged by rainwater. This time it was only slightly muffled by the fog.

"Bart!" she yelled, spitting rainwater. "Don't get on the bridge! It's too dangerous!"

His added weight might be enough to send them both over into the waters below. She could hear the rushing sound of the creek overflowing its banks.

"Can you move?" he asked, sounding closer.

How could he be? He was on the wrong side of the creek. Unless he'd crossed through the water itself. When she heard a snort and the sound of a hoof hitting board, all became clear.

"I'm all right," she called. "But I'm not sure about the pickup. If I open the door, it could go over."

"What about the window? Can you climb out?"

Josie judged the situation to be serious enough to try. The pickup's nose dipped down and to her right. And the rain was getting heavier.

"This will be a trick, but I'll see what I can do."

A testament to her trust in Bart. Had she been alone, she would never have tried this, at least not until she could see *something*. She'd been hoping all along that someone would come looking for her; it was the reason she'd been leaning on the horn.

Removing her seat belt, she immediately plowed forward into the steering wheel. The horn's blast accompanied a stomach-plunging dip and a splintering sound that zinged along her nerves.

"Carefully!" Bart barked.

"Like I had a choice," Josie muttered, though she was so glad not to be alone that she planned to throw her arms around Bart and kiss him.

Assuming she got out in one piece, that was.

Bracing a foot against the base of the floor shift, hanging onto the steering wheel with her right hand, Josie slowly inched herself into a standing position. Her head, shoulders and the top of her left arm cleared the opening. Rain drove into her face. Seeing was near-impossible.

"About a third of me is out," she said. "And I probably could hook a foot in the steering wheel to push up…but I don't know what will happen to the truck if I shift my weight too much."

"Are your hands free?"

"Uh, letting go wouldn't be my first option right now."

"Not even to catch a lifeline?"

Able to make out some movement on the bank several yards away, Josie imagined Bart was tying something to his saddle horn.

"You're going to rope me like a calf?"

"And brand you," he threatened. "Count out loud so I can place you. Be ready. When you get to 'five,' I'll throw. Pull the rope down and secure it around your waist."

A thrill of challenge shot through Josie. "Oh, yeah, that'll be easy."

"Ready?"

"As I'll ever be."

"One…two…"

A whirling sound muffled the count.

"…three…four…"

Josie braced herself.

"…five!"

A sharp whir cut through the fog and rain. The rope hit her shoulder and bounced off.

"*Almost* doesn't count in horseshoes!" she reminded him. "Too far to the right."

"So we'll try it again. I have all night. Tell me when you're ready."

Josie couldn't believe they were joking with each other. But maybe that was the trick to making this work—she being relaxed.

Only Bart could manage this, she thought, getting her to act so daringly with such calm. Seeing him with true clarity for perhaps the first time, she decided that, if he got her out of this mess, she would owe him everything, including the truth.

She owned a little more of it now. Bits and pieces of memory had been tumbling through her awakening mind ever since she'd set off. Unfortunately, the one thing she wanted most—the identity of the faceless man—still eluded her.

"Hey, Josie, what's going on?"

"Ready!" she called.

He tried again and managed to hit her other shoulder.

"Almost...but no cigar. You overcompensated."

"Third time's the charm," he promised.

Josie prayed so. She was wet and cold and her teeth were starting to chatter.

Bart repeated the ritual. "Four...five!"

This time she reached a hand up toward the soft whir and was rewarded when the loop fell over her arm. Quickly, she grabbed and dropped the rope over her shoulder.

"Got it, Bart! Hold on."

Carefully lifting her arm through, she found another handhold and adjusted the other side until the rope was around her waist. Quickly, she snugged it.

"We did it!" she yelled, suddenly boneless with relief. "Now what?"

"Now you climb out."

"Easy for you to say."

The rope between them grew taut and she got the idea—if the pickup did a nosedive, he meant the rope to keep her from going with it. Only she had to be free of the cab first.

She eased herself up with her hands...moving

very, very cautiously…balancing her weight as best she could.

Raising a leg, she found the steering wheel with her foot. And as she pushed up an inch at a time, Bart made certain the rope stayed taut, undoubtedly by backing up his horse exactly as he would if he'd just roped a calf.

"I'm setting a knee on the edge of the window," she told him even as she managed it.

She was hanging on to the rope with one hand, balancing herself on the vehicle with the other. But when she lifted her right foot free of the steering wheel, she kicked the horn and startled herself.

Only a small jump…but enough to set the pickup teetering.

Apprehension gripped her. As if goosed, she lunged herself out of the window and grabbed onto the rope, yelling, "Pu-u-ull!"

From behind her came a huge metal groan and a sharp set of splinters as the vehicle pushed farther through the broken bridge.

"Hang on!" Bart yelled as Josie took the plunge toward him.

The rope came up short, as did she into the side of the creek bank. The wind was knocked out of her, but up she came, turning and twisting through the muck. Bart didn't stop pulling until she was on the flat.

"Josie, say something!" he ordered.

"Let me spit out this mud first."

Groaning at the new wreckage of her body, she got to her knees. And then Bart's hands were hooked under her arms, pulling her up. Josie threw herself against him and somehow found his face for that kiss she'd promised herself.

She was filthy and he was dripping wet. When their lips touched, little rivulets of mud slid between their faces and mutual laughter ended the brief embrace.

Still, he touched fingers to her cheek and murmured, "Thank God I got here in time."

"No, Bart, thank *you* for rescuing me yet again."

"We've got to get you someplace warm and dry," he said, loosening the rope from her waist. "You're shaking."

Indeed, she was, but from relief or the chill or his touch, she didn't know. Maybe a combination of all three.

Glancing behind her, she noted the pickup was still dangling from the bridge. The headlights beamed through the thick weather, and she wondered how long it would remain in its precarious position before surrendering to the inevitable.

Rain drove at her, washing away the mud, but chilling her to the bone, as well.

"Josie, c'mon."

Bart was back in the saddle, holding out his hand. Josie took it and started to circle behind him to mount. He tugged, pulling her back where she'd started.

"In front," he said.

He slipped his foot from the stirrup so she could step into it. As she bounced up, he pulled her over his lap.

"Sorry about the saddle horn." He opened the front of his slicker. "Grab my waist and pull in close."

When she did as he told her, he wrapped the slicker around her as best he could and managed to secure a couple of the snaps. Josie luxuriated in being cradled by the man who had come to mean so much to her in so little time. Her wetness and his heat created steam together.

Later, she'd probably be able to laugh at that.

Head tucked against his chest, she asked, "Isn't this going to be awkward for you?"

"We're not going far. It would take too long to get back to the house, and the weather is bound to get worse. We need to get someplace dry and warm until it lets up."

"Where, then?"

"You'll see."

"Right," she muttered, knowing that with *her* night vision, that was highly unlikely.

Sighing, she settled in for the ride, content to let Bart take her where he would. Her world narrowed to the warm, moist cocoon he'd created for her.

Simple warmth soon progressed to something far more personal, however, and Josie thought she would gladly stay wrapped in Bart's arms forever.

And so a short while later, when he said, "We're almost there, but hang on tight," she did so gladly.

She never wanted to let go. Never wanted *him* to let go of her. Only she knew he would. She would let Bart down, and once his expectations were dashed, he would be relieved to be rid of her.

Chapter Thirteen

They began a slow ascent, moving in a serpentine pattern, Bart's announced goal a cave halfway up the rimrock.

Josie felt bereft when they passed under the overhang and he opened his slicker and helped her down. Then he dismounted and wrapped the slicker around her alone.

"Hang in a few more minutes and I'll have a fire going," he promised. "Then we'll get you nice and warm and dry."

She didn't tell him she was already glowing with warmth from their close contact. Instead, she tended Honcho, removing saddlebags and a bedroll, then the saddle itself. It seemed to her that Bart had come prepared for anything.

He quickly started the fire. Even the first small flames allowed Josie some idea of her surroundings. While the cave's mouth was large, it didn't cut back far into the rimrock. Deep enough to keep the weather from them, however, the cave proved cozy.

She spread open the bedroll near Bart, who was placing split wood over the flames.

"How did you know there would be firewood up here?" she asked.

"Tradition. My brothers and I always made certain we restocked."

Wondering when they'd last met here, she asked, "An old hangout for the Quarrels boys?"

"I guess you could call it that. This cave is the one place we left our disagreements behind," he said.

Making her think there had been many such disagreements between the brothers.

"It's good to have a place like that—something safe."

The fire was roaring now and Josie was already feeling drier. She sat cross-legged on the pad before the flames. Unbraiding her hair so that it would dry faster, she fluffed the long strands.

Bart joined her on the bedroll. Their knees touched and heat quickly spread from the point of contact. She shivered, but not from any chill this time. She didn't complain when Bart wrapped an arm around her back and pulled her closer. His hand began trailing up and down her arm in a rhythm that aroused her growing need for him.

Pulse thrumming, hoping she didn't sound too breathless, she admitted, "I haven't felt safe much lately...except when I'm with you."

"Could have fooled me. You haven't exactly been forthcoming."

"Your being a lawman is intimidating," Josie admitted. And then, determined to fulfill her silent promise, she said, "And I'm a thief."

The hand rubbing her arm stilled, but Bart didn't

say a word. He waited, as if expecting her to explain.

"That accident I told you about," she continued, dry-mouthed, "I, uh…I was driving a stolen truck." There, at last she'd said it!

"You're sure *you* stole the vehicle?"

"Who else?"

"The man you've been running from?"

"How do you know about…" Then it hit her—she'd only told one person. "Alcina."

"You've made a good friend in Alcina Dale, Josie. You can trust her just like you can trust me. So what will it be? Want to tell me what you didn't tell her?"

Those lawman's instincts were working overtime, and yet Bart didn't seem disgusted with her as Josie had feared he might. Now wasn't the time to hold back. She had to tell him everything she knew before she lost her nerve.

"I woke in the hospital to hear them talking about the stolen truck and how the authorities were running a check on my fingerprints." She got it all out in one big rush. "But I didn't remember doing anything wrong."

"So you ran."

"Which may be a habit with me," she warned him. "Give me a problem and there I go out the door."

"You're not running now."

"Not because I don't want to…but mostly because of you." Josie closed her eyes and said, "I've never met anyone like you, Bart." That was as close as she was going to get to making a declaration.

"That you remember," he amended.

"I know a lot of things by instinct, and I'm more sure of that than I am of my own name." She laughed at the irony. "Finally, it's coming back, but only in bits. A sorrel named Dreamsickle...and a cat named Peaches. A mother who died not too long ago—" for which she felt sorry even if she didn't remember her mom yet "—and a man who...may be trying to kill me, starting with the accident that brought me here and maybe including removing some boards from that bridge today. I think he shot at me and nicked Mack. And Peter...I—I even wonder what might have really happened to him."

Squeezing her arm, Bart admitted, "So do I."

"When I was in that stolen truck, I remember thinking he was after me...wasn't going to let me live...but I can't see his damn face so I can't do anything to stop him!"

Bart turned her in his arms so she was looking at him. He trailed her jaw with his thumb. "Josie, you're not going to die. I won't let it happen again."

"Again?" she echoed, confused. "My dying would be a first."

"I meant I won't lose another woman I love to violence."

"Love...?"

The word escaped her as softly as a breath. Before she could demand an explanation, Bart's mouth was covering hers, drawing from her emotions she hadn't been willing to face before.

She broke the kiss, protesting, "Bart, you don't really know anything about me."

"I know enough. You have a good heart...two good hearts if you count mine."

Josie was caught by the wonder of his declaration.

She searched his expression. His eyes. Little flames shot back at her, reflections of the firelight. She touched his face in wonder—so ruggedly handsome—from his broad cheekbones to the slight indentation in his chin.

Bart caught her wrist with his hand, her finger with his mouth. He sucked the tip, scraped his teeth across it, over the knuckles, along her wrist.

"How many fires are you willing to put out?" she asked shakily.

"As many as it takes."

Vaguely wondering if he meant the figurative fires set by her mystery man or the physical ones flaring between them with regularity, Josie kissed Bart. A new fire built in her fast, and she knew of only one way to put it out.

She was willing…eager…afraid….

But she had already determined that she was tired of being afraid.

And so, when Bart moved his hands over her more intimately, Josie welcomed his touch. When he began unbuttoning her damp shirt, she unbuttoned his, as well. Her fingers were stiff and uncooperative, but she persevered. And soon they were open to each other. His flesh burned her palms.

Bart cupped her unbound breasts and lowered his head to kiss the soft flesh. Josie arched into him, silently begging for more. When his mouth closed on a tender tip and suckled it, she let loose a sound that came straight from her soul. Lacing her fingers in his hair, she urged him on.

"Don't stop," she breathed.

She'd taken a chance on telling him the truth, so

why shouldn't she take a chance now? She had nothing left to lose and everything to gain.

Her memory...a real life to share...loving a man she could trust...

As crazy as it seemed, Josie was certain she was in love with Bart Quarrels. She had known him for so short a time, and yet they'd experienced more together in days than some people experienced in a lifetime.

"Josie," he murmured in her hair. "I want you."

"And I want you, Bart."

The truth. Instinct. Some things even a woman with no memory didn't have to question.

Bart didn't. He finished undressing her, then took her with a surety that left her no time for doubt. Joined before the fire, they made love until they fell asleep in each other's arms.

It was only afterward, when she awoke suddenly, her heart pounding in reaction to one of her frightening dreams, that the doubts started creeping back in. Bart continued to sleep, one leg thrown over her possessively, yet Josie wondered if she hadn't allowed her passions to cloud her mind. She hadn't been thinking straight.

No question remained in her mind about the bridge—enough boards had been removed to cause an accident. The perpetrator had known she'd gone to water the cows and that she would have to return the same way. Had known the weather would be against her. Had known her night vision was poor.

Will "Billy Boy" Spencer?

Will hadn't been there when she'd set off—he'd been chasing down strays, according to Frank. But

he could have been on his way back to the barn
when he'd spotted her.

Josie shivered despite the heat of the glowing em-
bers and Bart's body sheltering hers.

Bart was now bound to her, no matter the consequences. And there could be consequences…
maybe for him, as well as for her. If he got in the
way, who was to say that the man she loved
wouldn't become another target?

And what about his kids?

Josie's stomach did a familiar, unpleasant dance.

Dear Lord, what if she'd just put them all in danger?

FROM THE MOMENT they'd awakened together at
first light, Bart sensed Josie's distraction. Despite his
persuasiveness, she'd declined to make love again,
had insisted they get back before someone came out
to find them.

Though the sky was still gray as they set off, the
weather had lifted. Josie rode behind him this time,
touching him only as much as she needed to hang
on.

Why was she acting so oddly—so different from
the warm, loving, *trusting* woman he'd held in his
arms all night?

Bart put it to a reality check. She had other things
on her mind…like chasing down those elusive memories. He could give her space, if that's what she
needed, but only for the moment. When he got off
Honcho, he would take her in his arms and reassure
her.

But that proved impossible. By the time they got
back to the barn, a welcoming reception awaited

them. The hands had gathered and two of the horses were already saddled. Discussion stopped as Bart and Josie rode in.

Moon-Eye said, "We were just gonna form a search party."

They dismounted, and as the old hand looked from one to the other, his expression turned knowing. Frank seemed to be inspecting the toe of his boot, while Will stared at them, *his* expression strangely closed.

"Josie had an accident," Bart said, meeting Will's gaze directly. "The bridge gave. The pickup's still dangling over the creek."

The cowboy didn't so much as blink.

But Frank muttered something under his breath, and Moon-Eye sputtered, demanding to know more. Bart gave the bare details, leaving out anything personal. He was too aware of Josie's unusual silence on the matter. She was avoiding looking at any of the men, almost as if she were afraid to.

Bart didn't know his father was coming up behind him until he heard the old man mutter, "Another thing gone wrong...will it ever end?"

Before Bart could respond, his kids raced out of the house, Felice following. Lainey charged into him. "Dad, I thought something terrible happened to you!"

Hugging her in return, he said, "I'm fine, sweetheart, really. There was a problem with the truck and I only had one horse, so we found shelter and waited out the rain."

Even with the explanation, Lainey clung to him as if she feared another loss. He hugged her tightly.

"You're late, you know," Daniel informed him.

"The bus is long gone. I guess that means we don't have to go to school today."

Dryly, Bart said, "I'll drive you." His gaze went over his daughter's head to Josie, who finally spoke.

"Then you can drop me at Alcina's." Her expression was as closed as Will's. "I could use the day to myself."

Bart nodded. She needed some time alone, maybe some quality sleep. He'd give her a few hours. Then they were going to have another talk. He was going to get to the bottom of whatever was eating at her. He sensed more wrong than she'd already told him.

"Mr. Bart," Felice said, "a Sheriff Malone called. He said it was important."

"Thanks, Felice." Bart looked at Josie, who was more subdued than he'd ever seen her. "I need to get back to Malone before we leave."

"No problem."

"Miss Josie, you look like you could use some breakfast."

"Thanks, Felice, but I'm really not hungry."

Bart let go of his daughter. "Lainey, honey, get your things for school. You, too, Daniel."

"Yeah, Dad."

He started for the house. His father kept pace with him. "*Sheriff* Malone, huh? You tell him you got a job here."

"Malone's a friend, Pa," Bart said distractedly. "Don't worry, I'm not going anywhere."

"Mr. Emmett, remember your doctor's appointment," Felice said. "We should be leaving soon, as well."

"Nothing's wrong with my memory, woman!"

Bart took the opportunity to race inside, where he immediately called Malone.

"So what do you have?" he asked his old friend.

"One of the boys in San Miguel County recognized the photo—unofficially, you understand. It's not on the books. Her name's Joanne Walker. Her husband Randy came in last week, tried to get the department to issue a missing person bulletin on her."

Bart's heart stilled. *Josie's married?* "And?"

"A little conversation revealed something about a domestic squabble. Since we're not in the business of tracking down runaway wives, no one followed up."

Bart thanked him and hung up, then stood there staring at the telephone.

He'd just made love to another man's wife.

Had Josie—Joanne—suddenly remembered that part? Is that why she'd been acting so strangely? And if she did remember…then what else hadn't she told him?

Runaway wife—could the answer really be that simple?

Bart didn't know what to think.

JOSIE DIDN'T LIKE THE WAY Will stared at her, even after Bart went inside to return that call. Ignoring him, she scrambled into the SUV, half-expecting Will to follow her. Instead, he simply disappeared.

She took a deep breath to calm herself, but her stomach kicked up, anyway, and by the time Bart slid into the driver's seat, his kids in the back, she was thinking she should have agreed to that breakfast.

Bart started off immediately without saying a word to her. Instincts humming, Josie sensed something was wrong without him saying so. What now? Not that it mattered. She wouldn't be around long enough to find out what it was.

Certain that Will was the man who'd been stalking her, Josie knew she had to leave. He was too close for comfort. A rattler right in the Quarrelses' nest. If she disappeared, he would undoubtedly try to follow, and the danger would be over, at least for Bart and his kids. They would be safe, even if she was not.

Her memory was returning and soon she would know everything, including the whys and wherefores. *Then* she could deal with Will Spencer and with whatever she may have done to bring this situation on herself.

But first she had to get away.

"My dad's a real hero, isn't he?" Lainey suddenly piped up from the back seat. "Saving you from that bridge and all?"

Realizing the girl was talking to her, Josie turned to face Lainey. "Your dad is the bravest man I know," she said with all sincerity.

"But women can be brave, too, right? I mean, it's like your being a wrangler. We can do whatever we have a mind to," the girl said, echoing Josie's own sentiment of a few days ago. "Even be a hero."

Daniel snorted. "Fat chance you'll ever do anything heroic!"

"Shut up, dork!"

A lump sat squarely in Josie's throat as she turned to stare out the front window, somehow avoiding Bart as she did so. All *she* felt was scared, despite the admonitions she'd given herself over the past days. She might be tired of being afraid, but there seemed to be no helping it.

When Bart dropped her off with a terse "I'll be by later—we need to talk," Josie didn't say anything rather than lie.

Stomach roiling unpleasantly, she hurried into the kitchen, where Alcina had just brought in the leftovers from breakfast.

"Felice called and told me what happened. You're all right?" Alcina asked.

Josie fetched half a dry waffle and bit into it. "As good as can be expected under the circumstances, I guess."

"You'll feel better after you get some sleep."

Taking another bite to soothe her protesting stomach, Josie thought she might never feel better again. She was leaving the man she loved—how was she ever going to get over that?

Seeing that Alcina was about to go into the dining room, Josie beat her to it, saying, "I'll get the rest."

She was just in time to catch Tim Harrigan, who was about to leave the table that was otherwise empty. His eyes went wide when he saw her.

"You're not...working," he said. "Did you lose your job or something?"

"Something." Josie took a big breath. "Tim, I have a serious problem. That offer you made to get me out of here—"

He didn't let her finish. "When do you want to leave?"

Relief sluiced through her. "How soon can you be ready?"

"I just need to throw my stuff into a bag." Tim immediately whipped around toward the stairs.

"One thing." She caught his sleeve and stopped him. "I don't have the heart to leave Miss Kitty behind."

She felt as if she'd had the cat forever and couldn't fathom that she'd been willing to leave her before.

Tim's immediate frown was short-lived. His expression cleared and he shrugged. "I guess there's plenty of room for her carrier in the back of the pickup. Go—get your stuff together and I'll get mine. Meet you out back."

"Tim, thanks, really."

Josie wanted to say goodbye to Alcina, but the woman had disappeared from the kitchen. All for the best, she told herself. Alcina would probably try to stop her again, and Josie wasn't about to be talked out of leaving.

It took less than ten minutes to gather her things together. Bag in one hand, cat carrier in the other, Josie regretfully left the room she'd been glad to call home for a little while.

When she got outside, Tim was already waiting for her at his shiny red pickup. "That was fast," he said.

"I travel light."

Josie handed him her bag, which he threw into the back. But because Miss Kitty was getting agitated, scrunching against the rear of the carrier and growling, Josie figured she'd better take care of the frightened cat herself.

"It's going to be all right, sweetheart," she promised. "You'll see. I'm not going to dump you off anywhere like your last owner did.'' Carefully, she set the carrier next to her bag. ''You're coming with me, *wherever* I go.''

''Where is it you want to go?'' Tim asked.

Josie hadn't even considered where. ''What direction have you been heading in?''

''North.''

''Then north is fine with me.''

But first they needed to stop for gas.

Josie remained inside the truck, where she had time to think about what she was doing. Playing hero...leaving Bart out of the loop to protect him...just as Sara Quarrels had done.

Bart's late wife hadn't trusted him enough to help her handle that abusive father. Maybe Sara had been protecting that teenage girl, or maybe she'd been protecting Bart, but, according to Bart, Sara hadn't given him her trust.

Now Sara was dead, and Josie was about to repeat the same mistake.

A mistake.

The thought grew in her until she had to face it. She couldn't go off and leave Bart out. She couldn't do that to him, make him go through that hell a second time. He'd said he loved her, and even if she hadn't admitted as much, she loved him, too. And he was a lawman, after all, no matter that he wasn't wearing a badge. She had to stop running. She had to take her stand and fight. And she had to do it by Bart's side.

Meaning to tell Tim that she'd changed her mind, she left the truck.

''Hey, this is great, isn't it?'' Tim said, still

pumping gas. "You and me setting out on an adventure together."

Josie could hardly stand to look at him, he was so jazzed—kind of like a guy whose proposal had just been accepted. And when he unexpectedly hugged her, she shuddered inside, though she tried not to show it.

"Tim, please."

"What's wrong?" His face was mere inches from hers, his mouth pulled in a grin. "We're together now, just like it should be."

Her heart skipped a beat. "Together?"

"Right. You and me."

Oh, no! Josie shook her head. "I think I must have given you the wrong impression," she said gently, placing the blame on herself. "I consider you a friend. I'm not romantically interested in you."

His expression darkened. "After everything I've done for you…?"

Josie's pulse skittered, and, impulsively, she pulled away from him and reached for the cat carrier.

"What are you doing?" Before she could get her fingers around the handle, Tim grabbed her and twirled her around. She flew back against the side of the pickup.

A burst of pain in her abused side made her see stars.

And something else…

Open hand swung toward her. Contact! Her head snapped back. Frightened and confused, she stared at his face, red with fury.…

Chapter Fourteen

The memories came flooding back in a rush. Stunned, Josie blinked and forced herself through the fog of the past back to the very dangerous present. She needed her wits about her.

"I just wanted to make sure the cat was okay," Josie lied, her voice trembling over the sound of the animal's low growl. Heart pounding, grateful she hadn't announced her change in plans, she added, "You know, so the carrier doesn't slide around the back when we drive."

But her pretense didn't relieve his very real scowl. "The cat'll be fine just as she is. Get inside."

"Right," she said, forcing a smile and immediately hopping into the passenger seat.

Josie waited only until his back was turned. When he went to replace the nozzle, she hit the door lock, slid into the driver's seat and started the engine.

"Hey, Joanne, stop!" she heard him yell, even as she gunned the accelerator.

A fast check told her the street was clear. Josie turned toward the Curly-Q, glancing over her shoulder just long enough to see him trying to shove a grizzled old cowboy away from the door of an an-

cient pickup. She stepped on the gas and shot
through town, checking her rearview mirror every
few seconds, but she didn't see him following.

By the time she hit the washboard road, however,
a tiny speck in the distance had appeared in her mirror. The old cowboy must have put up a heck of a
fight, she thought, but he'd been no match for a
younger and angry man who had no compunctions
about pushing anyone around.

That shove had jogged her sleeping mind. Even
now the memories flowed.

*She turned the sorrel tight around the last barrel
and raced for home....*

*"Congratulations!" Randy said later, when she
was getting ready to leave. "That was the prettiest
ride I ever did see."*

*She smiled. "Thanks. That win meant a lot to me.
I dedicated the ride to my mom."*

*"I'd like to hear more about that. Over a beer,
maybe?"*

Bereft at her recent loss, she decided to tell him...

Her mom had died only weeks before, leaving
Josie the ranch where she'd raised and trained quarter horses, including a certain flaxen-maned sorrel
she'd given to Josie for her twenty-seventh birthday.

She'd ridden Dreamsickle on the barrel-racing circuit for nearly five years now. Modest winnings the
first year had doubled the second, and had grown
from there. The year before, Josie remembered,
she'd made enough winnings to qualify for the National Rodeo Finals...undoubtedly the reason Randy
had come after her.

On the Curly-Q property now, she glanced up into
the mirror, praying she'd see nothing. But the truck

was still there behind her. Heart racing, she gave the pickup more gas, speeding it over the washboard surface to put more distance between them. The vehicle vibrated violently, and she was aware of the cat carrier jouncing behind her.

"Sorry, Peaches," she muttered. *Peaches?* "Oh, my God!"

Miss Kitty *was* her cat, one she'd owned for years. How could she have missed that or the way the cat had reacted when "Tim" was around. Peaches had hated Randy from the first, but Josie had figured it to be nothing more than jealousy. But *Miss Kitty* had taken to Bart Quarrels. Obviously the cat had better instincts than she did when it came to men.

How could she have been so stupid? Josie wondered. So vulnerable?

Randy had played on her loneliness, and she'd let him. She'd needed someone after losing her only relative and had convinced herself that she cared for him enough to marry him. She'd let him take over the business side of their relationship, never suspecting that he'd paid off a bunch of gambling debts with her winnings.

But she'd found out.

When she wouldn't agree to sell her mother's ranch and horses to fund some money-making scheme of his, their argument had turned ugly and he'd hit her. Stunned, she'd been disbelieving. And then he'd apologized and begged her forgiveness, and she had been fool enough, needy enough, to believe him yet again.

Until he'd hit her a second time a few weeks later.

Josie shivered when she remembered the ugliness that had followed.

One last look before descending to the canyon floor assured her that he was still hot on her trail, that he still saw her as his meal ticket—alive or dead.

She took the hairpin curve too fast. Her stomach winged off in the opposite direction, scaring her into slowing before she had another accident.

Almost there, she told herself. Almost.

But when the house below came into view, she didn't see Bart's truck. He wasn't back from taking the kids to school yet. And no one was in sight but her equine escorts.

Juniper in the lead, the horses surrounded her as she hit the canyon floor. They stayed with her all the way to the house. Without even cutting the engine, she flew out of the truck and banged at the door.

"C'mon, c'mon!"

Then she remembered Felice mentioning a doctor's appointment. No one was home.

"Moon-Eye...Frank...Will! Anyone here?" she yelled at the top of her lungs as she raced back to the truck.

She glanced toward the rim. The pickup was already on its way down. Thinking to leave him his precious vehicle—perhaps he'd take it and leave— she grabbed her bag and cat carrier and ran for the barn.

Randy had been entitled to no more than a small settlement after such a short marriage. But the expensive new pickup hadn't been enough for him, and he'd tried to convince her to sign an agreement that would give him a share in her future assets, including the ranch and the now-valuable Dreamsickle. When she'd refused, he'd gone into a blind fury, had told her he'd kill the horse....

The very thought churned her stomach. She had no idea of whether or not he'd carried through with that threat. And what if he realized that she was alone now? Somehow, she was going to have to evade him.

"Peaches, you be quiet," she said, setting the bag and carrier behind the tack shed. "Don't let him know where you are!"

Tearing into the shed, she grabbed a halter and bridle, meaning to tack up the nearest horse and go where a vehicle couldn't follow. She was going to buy herself some time.

When the nearest horse proved to be none other than Juniper, hanging around, looking for a treat, she fought panic.

"I'll give you all the cake you can eat," she promised, seducing the green-broke mare with voice and hands. "If only you'll let me ride you."

Juniper neighed nervously and danced in place, but made no attempt to evade Josie, who slipped the bridle over the horse's head not a moment too soon.

The truck Randy had coerced the old cowboy into giving him was rolling to a stop near the pickup.

BART COULDN'T RID HIMSELF of the bad feeling he got when he stopped at Alcina's and found no Josie, no bag or clothes, no cat.

And then Alcina herself had come rushing in with a breathless tale of a stolen truck. Her boarder Tim Harrigan had coerced some hired ranch hand into giving it up so he could go after his own pickup, which had been headed in the general direction of the Curly-Q.

It hadn't taken a genius to figure Josie had been at the wheel…or that Tim Harrigan was, in fact, her husband Randy Walker and the man who'd been stalking her.

With a promise that he'd tell Alcina everything, Bart had flown out of the place and toward the ranch.

Good thing he'd caught up to the school bus and put his kids on board. Good thing he'd decided that talk with Josie couldn't wait.

She wasn't running away this time, he realized. She was running *to* him, giving him her full trust.

Now, if only he wasn't too late to prove that trust was well-placed….

JOSIE KNEW SHE HAD NO time to saddle up. Running her hands over Juniper to quiet the mare, she softly said, "I sure hope you trust me, girl."

Randy was lunging out of the old vehicle, yelling, "Joanne, you'd better show yourself now!" All traces of the charming, boyish, slightly shy man she'd thought to be Alcina's boarder had vanished.

Quietly, Josie threw a looped rope over her shoulder and sneaked Juniper toward an old tractor tire. She lined the mare up next to it.

"Joanne!" Randy yelled again even as Josie climbed up on the tire and used it as a mounting block.

The rubber sprang a little as she carefully threw a leg over the horse. And as her weight settled on

Juniper's back, the mare snorted and feinted to the right and Randy turned and spotted them both.

"Joanne, don't be stupid! I don't *want* to hurt you."

As if she could ever believe his intentions again. "What did you do to Dreamsickle?"

"Your damn mare is fine! But we need to make a deal," he said, his tone desperate.

Praying that he wasn't lying about her horse, she asked, "How big are *these* gambling debts?"

If that was his excuse. Keeping him talking would buy her some time. Maybe the men would come back from whatever pasture they were working in. Besides, she needed to figure out how to get past him and down to the creek.

"I owe enough that they'll hurt me bad if I don't pay up," he wheedled. "Please, Joanne, get me out of this jam and I won't ever ask you for anything more, I promise."

He was doing his best to con her again. But Josie remained untouched.

"Randy, I'll never give you another thing. Not trust or pity or money. And I'm not alone anymore. Bart Quarrels is a lawman, you know, and he has your number. So why don't you just get out of here while you still can?"

"Bitch!" he screamed. "You keep underestimating me! I want that money because I *earned* it, not because there's someone after me. And there's no one here to save you this time!"

"Why, Randy? What did I ever do to you that you would see me dead?"

"Killing you wasn't my first option," he admitted. "I fell for you, Joanne, I really did. I wanted your money and you. That's why I followed you to Silver Springs when you ditched the hospital. Your having amnesia gave me another chance at making us work. I figured even if your memory came back, I could convince you that you got some things wrong.''

He was delusional, but she wanted to hear it all. ''What about setting up Peaches in that abandoned building? I remember now…you came and took her so I would agree to meet you to get her back…''

But when he'd turned on her and had taken her keys, she'd run from him in fear for her life.

''I was only trying to scare you—same with my shooting at you on that big bay. I thought you would turn to me, but you went to another man instead and left me no choice.''

Sensing she'd stalled him about all she could, Josie collected the mare with steady hands and firm legs and mentally prepared herself for the coming physical confrontation.

''So you tried to get me, but you killed Peter Dagget instead.''

''Who? What are you babbling about?''

''The kid riding this horse yesterday morning.''

''You're hallucinating, Joanne. I meant the bridge.''

Figuring he was trying to exonerate himself, she said, ''Killing me won't get you what you want.''

'I want your money, Joanne, with or without you. You seem to have forgotten that if you accidentally die, I get everything, including the insurance.''

''I changed my will,'' she bluffed.

''You never did learn to lie well.''

Even as he reached into the back of the pickup,

his threat hit home. Furious, Josie rode straight for him, letting the looped rope drop down her arm. Noticeably startled by her sudden rush, Randy jumped away from the vehicle, holding the rifle he'd snagged.

Praying Juniper wouldn't rear up, Josie went straight for him even as he raised the weapon. She grasped the loops of rope and swung the bundle with all her might. The rope splayed open and caught him hard in the face and chest and he went flying all in a tangle, giving her precious seconds for a getaway.

As she turned the horse tight around the pickup, she heard him yell after her, "You just sealed your own fate!"

BART COULDN'T BELIEVE his eyes. Starting his descent to the canyon, he saw Josie temporarily disarm her husband and ride off bareback on Juniper. But Randy Walker wasn't down for the count. He regrouped, freed himself of the rope, grabbed his rifle and slid into the red pickup. Within moments, Walker was after Josie.

And *he* was after Walker, Bart thought grimly, thankful he'd brought his rifle.

What was going on? Why did Walker want to kill his own wife?

Knowing Josie was married had stalled him temporarily, but Bart had recovered from the shock. He'd seen her heart, even if she hadn't yet given it to him fully. Besides, he trusted her and instinct told him she was an innocent in this dangerous game of Walker's. And the lawman in him was determined to bring the bastard to justice.

JOSIE KNEW RANDY was behind her—she could hear his pickup's powerful engine. But as long as he was driving, he couldn't shoot at her, and as long as she kept riding through areas that wouldn't make her a target, he would keep driving.

She meant to get to the creek near the bridge and cross it where it was too deep for a motorized vehicle of any kind to venture.

Since Randy had put the bridge itself out of commission, that would leave him on the wrong side of the creek. She then would have options—like crossing through the pasture that would take her over the old mine field to the road back to Silver Springs.

If she did that, though, she would worry about what Randy might be up to—whom he might fool and then hurt in his effort to get away. Randy Walker was *her* problem, Josie decided. She couldn't let him loose on unsuspecting people.

The bridge didn't come too soon for her. It lay ahead, looking every bit a child's broken and abandoned toy. Amazingly, the pickup still clung to its precarious perch over the creek.

Time to get across where Randy couldn't get to her.

Slowing, she found a path down to the water, but the mare shied from the challenge.

"C'mon, Juniper, you can do this."

She sweet-talked the roan for all she was worth, rubbing one hand over the damp neck to calm her. She tried again. Juniper balked. Josie was getting nervous—that engine was closing in on them.

Calling on a little trickery, she reined the mare in a full circle and goosed her at the path. Juniper moved out and down, but she threw her head and snorted indignantly, as if telling Josie she knew exactly what her rider had just done.

The creek itself was even more threatening to the mare, who backed away from the water's edge and squealed. Josie approached it again and again, but ready for her tricks this time, Juniper was getting more and more agitated, even bucked her a few times.

Josie stopped dead and let the horse stare at the moving water as precious seconds ticked away. She heard the engine move up on them, knew exactly when it slowed. Her heart raced. Exposed as she was, she made a perfect target.

Centering herself, Josie waited quietly and felt Juniper relax under her. Above, the vehicle stopped.

No more time to wait. Now or never.

Gathering her will and tightening her legs, she pushed the mare forward, slapping her on the rump. Before Juniper could think about whirling around or bucking again, they were flying through the water. Not that the mare stopped on the other side—she shot straight up the embankment, scrabbling against ground that churned under her hooves.

Josie lay across the mare's neck in an effort to make the climb easier.

And to make herself a smaller target.

She awaited the whine of a bullet that never came. Instead, she heard the pickup moving again. Now they were above the creek, but it took her a moment to settle Juniper. When Josie glanced back, the vehicle was starting to cross the bridge.

What in the world did Randy think he was doing? He could only go a little more than halfway.

He rolled to a stop a yard from the maw and the dangling old pickup. When he alighted, his rifle was in hand. It dawned on her that he was going for the higher elevation of the bridge—better to take aim at her—and the land here was mostly open.

About to make a run for it, Josie heard another engine coming from the direction of the house. She craned around as Bart's SUV pulled into sight. Relief warred with worry, for she was certain the man she loved didn't know what he was up against.

In hopes of distracting her ex-husband, she shouted, "Give it up, Randy!"

"I'm not done yet, Joanne. I'm not doing any more jail time."

Not that she'd known he'd ever been in jail...

But Randy wasn't getting off the bridge the way he'd come, either, Bart's vehicle making an effective roadblock.

The lawman crawled out the safer passenger side, yelling, "Josie, get the hell out of here!"

"Bart, he's armed!"

"That makes two of us. Now go!"

Randy turned his attention to Bart, using his own pickup as a barricade. Josie couldn't just leave, but there was nothing she could do except watch, heart in her throat.

"Turn yourself in, Walker, and it'll go easier on you."

Josie's eyes widened. Bart *knew.* How?

"I'll see you in hell first!" came Randy's reply. "It'll be a pleasure to kill a wife-stealing bastard like you!"

He aimed and shot, the whine shattering Josie's

composure. "Leave him alone, Randy—it's me you want!"

"Josie, go!" Bart yelled again.

Which she ignored. Moving a nervous Juniper closer to the bridge, she took the same tone she'd use on a horse she was trying to seduce. "C'mon, Randy. We can work something out."

Her last words were drowned in an exchange of gunfire. If this kept up, someone was bound to get shot. She feared it might be Bart. She dismounted and dropped Juniper's reins to the ground.

"Randy, please," she said, moving onto the bridge, "I'll do whatever you want of me. You have those papers for me to sign in the truck, don't you?"

"What if I do?"

"Get them and I'll sign now. Then you can leave and no one has to go to jail."

"Why should I believe you?"

"What have you got to lose?" Josie asked, stopping mere feet from the broken section of the bridge. "Try me. Get the papers."

She would sign anything if that would make him go away without hurting anyone. The authorities could deal with him later—assuming they could find him once he got his hands on the money. All she wanted was for her and Bart to walk away from this alive, and Randy was too desperate to let that happen, unless Bart could take him out first. She wasn't willing to take the chance.

"Josie, what the hell are you trying to prove?" Bart demanded.

"I want this to end so that we all come out alive!" she yelled back. "Hold your fire, Bart. He wants my money, he can have it!" Softer, in that practiced seductive voice she normally reserved for horses and cats, she told her ex-husband, "I don't care about the money enough to let anyone get killed over it, Randy, not even you."

Which was true. Josie's pulse threaded unevenly as she waited for him to make up his mind.

"No tricks or I'll kill you both," he promised.

"No tricks."

Randy slipped inside his vehicle long enough to take a portfolio from behind the driver's seat. "Dot every i and cross every t," he warned her.

He aimed and carefully tossed the large folder over the abandoned pickup. She caught it, quickly moved away from the deathtrap and pulled out the contents, including the pen he'd so thoughtfully provided. If she had signed these papers in the first place, Randy would never have taken her keys, forcing her to steal that truck to get away from him. She never would have had that accident. *She never would have met Bart.*

Undoubtedly, that would have been better for him and his family. She glanced over to Bart where he waited at his vehicle, rifle lowered. He didn't look happy, but she didn't care. Money just didn't matter enough to chance any of them.

After signing the papers, every last one, she bundled them back inside, then moved closer to the danger zone.

"Signed, sealed and delivered," she said, tossing the folder straight to her ex.

Randy reached out too eagerly. The portfolio hit his hand and went flying back at her, falling short and onto the tilted hood of the abandoned pickup that dangled between them.

"Hell!" he yelled.

Desperate, Randy lunged after the promise to his fortune, not watching where he stepped.

The crack as loud as a gunshot made Josie jump back, even as she realized a rotted board beneath his foot had given way. Randy yelled again and tried to regain his balance, but he was toppling forward with increasing velocity.

Bart was already scrambling over his SUV as Randy threw out his hands in front of him. The smack of their slamming into the old truck echoed along the creek.

Gaze caught by the unfolding horror before her, Josie retreated farther even as Bart raced toward the disaster.

"Bart, no!" she yelled, fearing for him, knowing there was no saving Randy now. He might take Bart with him.

A bird landing on the doomed pickup would have rocked it. Randy's weight forced devastation. His scream was lost in the agony of screeching metal and cracking boards.

Bart was there, balancing awkwardly on the unsafe precipice, reaching out, clawed hand snagging the back of Randy's jacket. Too late. The force of the falling body ripped the material free. Bridge, truck and man raced to the waters below.

Through it all, Josie held her breath until she was sure Bart was safe.

Only then, when the air grew thick with the stillness of death, did Josie stumble closer to see.

Below, the pickup lay in the creek like a turtle flipped onto its shell. Next to it, a hand floated up to the surface. For a moment, the portfolio lingered in the still fingers.

Then it was sucked away by the greedy current, along with Randy's life.

REFUSING A RIDE in Bart's pickup, a stunned Josie returned to the barn the way she'd come—but on a much more experienced Juniper, who took the creek with little more than eye-rolling and snorting. Bart had beaten them back, she noted, though he was nowhere in sight. As promised, Josie rewarded the mare with a bucket of cake.

Then she went to fetch her beloved Peaches, sat in the dirt behind the tack shed with the cat in her lap and had herself a good cry.

She cried for her mother's death. For the lonely innocent she had been. For Randy wasting his life on something so unimportant as money. For finding the love of her life one man too late.

Bart hated violence and she had brought it straight to his door.

She didn't know how long he stood there, watching her, before he said, "I called the sheriff's office. They're sending a team out to recover the body." He cleared his throat nervously. "I'm sorry for your loss."

A quick look up showed her his closed expression. Closing himself off from her? Because she'd given him her trust too late?

"Loss?" She shrugged. "If only it were that simple. In a way, I'm responsible for Randy's death."

Bart leaned over and pulled her up to her feet, while a purring Peaches hugged her, claws catching in her denim jacket.

"You didn't do this," he said.

She clung to the cat tightly. "I should have given him what he wanted in the first place…as part of the divorce settlement."

"Divorce?" Bart couldn't hide the relief in his expression as he said, "He would have come back for more."

Josie started. He hadn't known everything, then. He'd thought she was a married woman. "How long have you known about Randy?"

"That call I made to Deputy Malone this morning…"

He went on to explain about the photo and Randy's attempt to get the police to find her.

"He thought he could get away with anything," Josie said. "I divorced him. He wouldn't let me be. I put a restraining order on him. He ignored it. So I just decided to disappear for a while, hoping he'd give up and go away. Instead, he found me. He didn't even need the help from the authorities." She sighed. "You knew about that and you didn't say anything. Talk about trust."

"I made a mistake and I knew it," Bart admitted. "That's why I came back so fast. I wanted to have that talk. To tell you."

Josie nodded. Not that it made any difference now. She had a life waiting for her elsewhere. And he had his family to worry over.

Bart cupped her cheek and brushed the moisture from it with his thumb. "If you were through with Walker, Josie, then why so many tears?"

She hedged. "He was a human being and I was close to him for a little while. I did care about him until I knew what he was. And…"

"And?" he prompted.

"And I'm sad to be leaving."

Bart scowled at her. "You're leaving? Why?"

"I know who I am now. And I'm not who you thought I was."

"You're so much more. You mean the world to me, Josie. I don't know what I would have done if something had happened to you."

"Or me if it had been you," she admitted, a lump in her throat. "I had to stop him before he hurt you."

"What you did was crazy and smart and very brave. Walker's own greediness did him in."

Josie nodded. "He admitted being responsible for the bridge. He'd given up trying to scare me back into his arms and got serious."

"And got caught in his own trap."

"Poetic justice," she murmured.

"A good thing for him. If I had gotten my hands on him, I would have ripped him apart."

"After saving his life? You tried your best, Bart. Why?"

"Like you said, he was a human being. And I guess I'll always be a lawman."

They stared at each other for a moment. Josie felt tears threatening her once more, and to cover, she stooped to put the cat back in her carrier.

"Are you really going to leave me?" he asked.

"You'll find a new wrangler."

"But I can't replace Josie Wales."

Rising, she blinked her tears away. "There is no Josie Wales."

"The hell there isn't—"

"She's a figment of my amnesia."

"I'm looking at her. She's here," Bart said, patting the left side of his chest. "And here." He touched hers, making her heart beat faster. "I don't want to lose her. Don't run away from *me*, please."

She didn't want to run. She was tired of it. She wanted to stay put with a man she loved. Have a sense of belonging. A big family, something she'd never had.

"I love you, Bart Quarrels...but what about your kids?"

"When they get to know you better, they'll love you, too." As if certain she was softening, Bart grinned at her and pulled her into his arms. "Any other objections?"

Josie's pulse thrummed even as she said, "I did rush into things with Randy. Not that I think you're anything like him," she hastened to add.

"Then we'll take it as slow as you need," Bart promised, his face drawing closer to hers, one hand traveling down the small of her back.

Suddenly breathless, she echoed, "Slow?"

She thought he would take forever getting his mouth to hers. "Slow," he murmured as their lips touched and that wayward hand strayed even lower.

Josie gave herself over to the moment. She always had wanted a man with a slow hand....

Epilogue

A bolt of electricity charged through Josie as she and Dreamsickle shot across the arena, horse and rider moving together, of one mind. And she anticipated every second of the competition before it even happened.

The flaxen mane whipping along a sorrel neck…

…the tight, fast turns around three barrels…

…and the rapid flight to the finish.

Josie felt the rush of victory when she heard her time and knew that she had won the event. Her mouth pulling into a wide grin, she lifted her hat and tossed it into the air.

That grin was still tugging at her lips later when she joined Bart and his kids outside the arena.

"Congratulations," Bart said and gave her a chaste peck on the cheek.

"That was awesome, Josie!" Daniel declared.

"I got a ton of photographs of your ride!" Lainey said.

"I'm looking forward to seeing them," Josie told the girl. "Maybe you can help me add them to my scrapbook?"

"Sure," Lainey agreed, "if you can give me some barrel-riding lessons. Please?"

Josie grinned wider. "Deal."

It had been only a few weeks and Bart's kids were already taking to her.

"Hey, I'm starving!" Daniel complained. "Are we ever gonna chow down?"

Bart dug into his jeans pocket and pulled out two tens. "Knock yourselves out. We'll meet you over by the Ferris wheel in half an hour."

The siblings flew away from the adults and into the crowd.

"Looks like the plan's working," Bart said.

"It's a great plan."

She and Bart were really getting to know each other, solidifying their relationship. By their including his kids, Daniel and Lainey both were accepting her presence in their lives without trauma. By the time she and Bart were ready to take the next step—marriage—Josie hoped the kids would care for her as much as she already did for them.

Suddenly realizing Bart seemed distracted—he was staring into the crowd around them—she nudged him. "Hey, where'd you go?"

"Just looking for someone who isn't here."

"Your brother?"

"Yeah, I was kind of hoping I might spot Chance…"

They'd learned that Chance had been expected to ride in a couple of events the next night, but that he had withdrawn from both. Though she didn't really know Bart's brother, Josie vaguely remembered him from the rodeo circuit as being very focused, very competitive. His withdrawing was kind of weird.

"You miss him, don't you?"

"Part of me does," Bart admitted. "And we could use his help back at the Curly-Q."

They could sure use help from someone, Josie thought, what with all the bad luck the ranch had been having. Bad luck including a death. She would never forget Peter Dagget.

"Pa says Chance has never stayed away for such a long time before," Bart added. "He's worried."

"You are, too."

"Me, too." Then, squeezing her waist, he said, "Let's find someplace to be alone for a few minutes before we have to go find my kids."

"Sounds like a plan," Josie murmured, her pulse skittering as she considered how enjoyable a few minutes of privacy could be with the man she loved.

ALONE...

Chance Quarrels was nursing a beer, sitting alone in a bar on the other side of town from the arena. He'd already withdrawn from the saddle bronc and bareback competitions that would be held the next night. He had a lot on his mind—too many distractions to believe he could have a safe ride—and no one to talk to.

A couple of cowpokes he knew entered laughing and joking. They grew quiet when they spotted him and sat at the opposite end of the bar, their backs to him.

He was getting used to being a pariah.

Suddenly the beer tasted flat and Chance pushed himself away from the bar.

Not much longer, he told himself. *Then it would be over.*

He even had a place to go to wait it out.

* * * * *

Don't miss Chance Quarrels's story in

THE LONE WOLF'S CHILD,

the second book in the

SONS OF SILVER SPRINGS

trilogy by Patricia Rosemoor.
Coming next month from Harlequin Intrigue

You loved Gayle Wilson's original series,
MEN OF MYSTERY, *so much
that we've brought it back!*

HARLEQUIN®

INTRIGUE®

presents

Coming in April 2000
#561 HER PRIVATE BODYGUARD
A new story by Gayle Wilson

Former CIA operative Grey Sellers is a man with
deadly secrets. But when his skills are needed to
protect reluctant heiress Valerie Beaufort, Grey
knows his true identity will soon be revealed. For
Valerie's life is on the line, and the only way to
assure her safety is to call in old favors....

Look for **MORE MEN OF MYSTERY**
available at your favorite retail outlet.

HARLEQUIN®

Makes any time special ™

Visit us at www.romance.net   HIMMM

Looking For More Romance?

Visit Romance.net

Look us up on-line at: http://www.romance.net

Check in daily for these and other exciting features:

Hot off the press

View all current titles, and purchase them on-line.

What do the stars have in store for you?

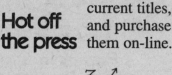

Horoscope

Hot deals

Exclusive offers available only at Romance.net

Plus, don't miss our interactive quizzes, contests and bonus gifts.

PWEB

HARLEQUIN®

I N T R I G U E®

presents

LOVERS UNDER COVER

Dangerous opponents, explosive lovers—
these men are a criminal's worst nightmare
and a woman's fiercest protector!

A two-book miniseries
by RITA Award-nominated author

Carly Bishop

They're bad boys with badges, who've
infiltrated a clandestine operation. But to
successfully bring down the real offenders,
they must risk their lives to defend the
women they love.

In April 2000 look for:

NO BRIDE BUT HIS (#564)
and
NO ONE BUT YOU coming soon!

Available at your favorite retail outlet.

HARLEQUIN®
Makes any time special ™

Visit us at www.romance.net   HILUC

Mother's Day is Around the Corner...
Give the gift that celebrates Life and Love!

Show Mom you care by presenting her with a one-year subscription to:

For only **$4.96**—
That's **75% off the cover price.**

This easy-to-carry, compact magazine delivers 4 exciting romance stories by some of the very best romance authors in the world.

Plus each issue features personal moments with the authors, author biographies, a crossword puzzle and more...

A one-year subscription includes 6 issues full of love, romance and excitement to warm the heart.

To send a gift subscription, write the recipient's name and address on the coupon below, enclose a check for $4.96 and mail it today. In a few weeks, we will send you an acknowledgment letter and a special postcard so you can notify this lucky person that a fabulous gift is on the way!

Yes! I would like to purchase a one-year gift subscription (that's 6 issues) of WORLD'S BEST ROMANCES, for only $4.96. I save over 75% off the cover price of $21.00.   MDGIFT00

This is a special gift for:

Name _____

Address _____ Apt# _____

City _____ State _____ Zip _____

From _____

Address _____ Apt# _____

City _____ State _____ Zip _____

Mail to: HARLEQUIN WORLD'S BEST ROMANCES
P.O. Box 37254, Boone, Iowa, 50037-0254 Offer valid in the U.S. only.

WHAT'S SEXIER THAN A COWBOY?
Three cowboy *brothers!*

HARLEQUIN®
INTRIGUE®
presents

A new trilogy by
bestselling author

PATRICIA ROSEMOOR

On a mission to save the family ranch and
make peace with each other, the Quarrels
boys are back in Silver Springs—but a
hidden danger threatens all they hold
dear, including their very lives!

Coming Spring 2000:

March: #559 HEART OF A LAWMAN
April: #563 THE LONE WOLF'S CHILD
May: #567 A RANCHER'S VOW

Available at your favorite retail outlet.

HARLEQUIN®
Makes any time special ™

Visit us at www.romance.net

HISOSS

Harlequin is having a

Heatwave

Featuring *New York Times* Bestselling authors

LINDA LAEL MILLER
BARBARA DELINSKY
TESS GERRITSEN

Watch for this incredible trade paperback collection on sale in May 2000.

Available at your favorite retail outlet.

HARLEQUIN®
Makes any time special ™

Visit us at www.eHarlequin.com

PHEAT

COMING NEXT MONTH

#561 HER PRIVATE BODYGUARD by Gayle Wilson
More Men of Mystery

New heiress Valerie Beaufort was forced to depend on Grey Sellers for protection. She didn't want a bodyguard, especially one with smoky silver eyes and a secret past he refused to reveal. But with danger stalking Valerie, neither of them could deny the attraction they shared—and Valerie couldn't resist the lure of a man of mystery....

#562 PROTECTING HIS OWN by Molly Rice

Forced to flee with her best friend's twin children, Katelynn Adams took on a new identity and began a new life. Until Joe Riley arrived with the news that Katelynn and the kids were no longer safe. Life on the run led to shared dangers and shared passions, but if Joe was the twins' father, would Katelynn lose her children...or gain a family?

#563 THE LONE WOLF'S CHILD by Patricia Rosemoor
Sons of Silver Springs

Chance Quarrels's return to Silver Springs brought back more than old memories for Prudence Prescott. Someone was out to silence Chance, and when physical intimidation didn't work, Prudence and her daughter became the villain's pawns. Chance knew he had to save the only woman he'd ever loved. What he didn't know was that he'd also be saving *his* child.

#564 NO BRIDE BUT HIS by Carly Bishop
Lovers Under Cover

Detective Ann Calder found undercover cop JD Thorne wounded and without memory. Hiding out as husband and wife, Ann could only hope that JD's instincts of friend and foe were correct. Until JD could recall who had attacked him and the crucial evidence he had found, he and Ann weren't safe—and unless they could put some distance between them, neither were their hearts.

Visit us at www.romance.net